THE RHAPSODY OF LOVE

Orlena could hardly believe her eyes.

There, standing in front of her, was her new Guardian, the man her late father had chosen to protect her large fortune.

But this was no elderly, solicitous friend of her father's. Nor was he a stranger to Orlena.

This was the very man she had met the night before at the posting inn—the man who swept her into his arms and thrilled her senses with a kiss of passion.

BARBARA CARTLAND

Bantam Books by Barbara Cartland
Ask your bookseller for the books you have missed

Barbara Cartland
The Rhapsody of Love

BANTAM BOOKS · TORONTO · NEW YORK · LONDON

THE RHAPSODY OF LOVE
A Bantam Book | April 1977

ISBN 0–553–10971–5

Published simultaneously in the United States and Canada

Bantam Books are published by Bantam Books, Inc. Its trade-
mark, consisting of the words "Bantam Books" and the por-
trayal of a bantam, is registered in the United States Patent
Office and in other countries. Marca Registrada, Bantam
Books, Inc., 666 Fifth Avenue, New York, New York 10019.

PRINTED IN THE UNITED STATES OF AMERICA

Author's Note

Astley's Royal Amphitheatre was rebuilt for the third time and opened in 1804 as "the handsomest pleasure haunt in London."

The interior was very impressive with the largest stage in London framed by a proscenium arch as high as the gallery above three tiers of boxes. It was lit by a huge chandelier containing fifty patent lamps.

Grand scenic displays were the fashion and the Circus produced one staggering spectacle after another. Later "The Battle of Waterloo" with two hundred horses taking part vied with the open-air presentation of the same theme at Vauxhall Gardens.

The Amphitheatre continued until the end of the last century when it was pulled down by the Ecclesiastical Commissioners in 1893.

The façade of the Bushel at Newmarket can still be seen, but the interior has been gutted.

Children continued to die in the streets and Workhouses and despite the efforts of a few Churches like St. James's, Westminster, Foundling Hospitals, and several Acts of Parliament, it was nearly fifty years before there was a noticeable improvement.

Chapter One

1803

The Senior Partner of Thorogood, Harrow and Chesnet cleared his throat and taking off his gold-rimmed spectacles put on the pair he always used for reading.

He glanced at the two young people sitting opposite him. Then speaking in a tone which he considered suitably funereal he said:

"I will now read you your father's will."

He took a small piece of paper from the impressive black leather case he had placed beside him on the desk, and clearing his throat once again he said:

"You are both already aware of your father's wishes as regards the wearing of mourning, and that he desired no-one to attend his funeral."

The young man to whom he was speaking stirred restlessly in his chair.

He was thinking that when this old bore had finished informing them of what they already knew, he would tell his sister, who was sitting beside him, that the reason for the will being so small was that his father was economising on paper!

Mr. Thorogood's next words confirmed what he was thinking as he continued:

"Your father did not ask me to draw up his will but wrote it out himself, and it was witnessed by two servants. It is, however, completely legal—if slightly unorthodox."

Orlena glanced towards her brother, knowing how much it irritated him when people took a long time to come to the point. She was aware that he was annoyed and only hoped he would allow Mr. Thorogood to finish the ceremony on which he had insisted before making some excuse to leave the room.

It was obvious that Terry had found the bleak funeral service almost intolerable. It had in fact considerably depressed her also, although she told herself she had expected nothing else.

Only her father would have insisted on the cheapest possible coffin and that there should be no mourners, that no-one should wear black and no Service be held inside the Church.

The coffin had been carried to the grave, where the Vicar had read the Burial Service; then it had been lowered into the ground by a few old retainers, after which they had walked away.

She was quite certain that her father's insistence on there being no mourners was to ensure that no-one should expect to receive any hospitality after the service was over.

She was equally certain that if they had disobeyed his wishes and notified the few relatives who lived nearby that he was dead, he would have risen from the grave to denounce them!

She too found it hard to attend to Mr. Thorogood.

Ever since her father had died she and her brother had been trying to think of how they could live and, most important of all, how they could keep Weldon Park.

"It is my home," Terry had said fiercely, "and has

been in our family for more than two centuries. I am
damned if I will give it up!"

"I am afraid there will be little alternative," Orlena had replied quietly. "It is crumbling into the
ground! The roof has not been repaired for years, and
you know that when the last ceiling fell in the Picture
Gallery I told Papa about it and he just said: 'Let it
fall!'"

"The Picture Gallery!" Terry said scoffingly.
"What pictures are left have been ruined by the damp
and faded by the sun, or they have just fallen out of
their frames through neglect."

"I know! I know!" Orlena cried. "Do not torture
yourself! There was nothing we could do, as you
well know. And I am afraid there will be little we can
do in the future."

"How are we going to live?" Terry asked.

Orlena had not replied.

The question had in fact haunted her when she had
gone to bed and it seemed to be repeated over and over
in her mind all through the days before the funeral.

She knew how bitter it would be for Terry, as
the new Baronet, to have to sell the lands which had
belonged to the Weldons since the reign of Queen
Elizabeth, but what alternative was there?

They could hardly live—or starve as they were
now doing—on what could be shot on the Estate.

"Rabbit again!" Terry had exclaimed only yesterday, and she had replied apologetically:

"The butcher will not give us any credit, and although it is the wrong time of the year to be eating
rabbit there is nothing else."

Terry's lips had tightened. He knew as well as she
did that they had no money with which to buy food.

It was only a question of time before he could no
longer afford to shoot what game there was to be
found in the fields, which were unploughed, and the
woods, which were rife with vermin.

Mr. Thorogood was holding the piece of paper at

an angle to catch the light coming in through the Library window.

It was a task which was made more difficult by the fact that the window needed cleaning.

Glancing at it, Orlena saw that the curtains were in tatters and knew that however skilfully she mended them they would not hold together any longer.

" 'This is my last will and testament,'" Mr. Thorogood read aloud, "'and I Sir Hamish George Northcliffe Weldon, fifth Baronet of Weldon Park in the County of Yorkshire, being of sound mind leave everything I possess and my whole Estate divided equally between my two children, Terence Northcliffe and Orlena Alexandra.'

"It is signed and witnessed," Mr. Thorogood finished.

"Is that all?" Terence asked, his voice rather loud, so that Mr. Thorogood started.

"Yes, Sir Terence. Your father was brief and to the point."

"The point in which I am interested," Terry said, "is what has he left? I presume there will be enough to pay your fee?"

"There will be more than enough, Sir Terence," Mr. Thorogood replied in a reproving tone.

He considered he was being hurried over a task which he invariably enjoyed because essentially he played the leading role.

"I am certainly glad to hear that," Terry remarked, "although I doubt if there will be anything left to improve the condition of this poor-house."

"Terry!" Orlena exclaimed rebukingly.

She was always afraid that her impulsive brother would express his mind too freely and she felt it would be unfortunate if Mr. Thorogood should go away with the wrong impression.

The Solicitor put the piece of paper carefully away in his leather brief-case.

"Well?" Terry asked almost truculently. "Are you

going to tell us the worst or have we to wait until you have added up the few pence which my father secreted away in the Bank?"

He paused to add bitterly:

"You know as well as I do that my sister and I seldom saw a penny-piece of anything he owned."

Orlena thought that Mr. Thorogood's dried-up face softened for a moment as if in fact he understood what they had been through. Then he said in his usual pompous tone:

"It is a little early, Sir Terence, as you must be aware, to give you an accurate accounting of your father's possessions, but I assure you my office will be making a complete inventory as quickly as possible."

"It can hardly take long!"

Terry spoke so contemptuously that once again Orlena reached out to put a hand on his arm, before saying quietly in her soft voice:

"Will you tell us, Mr. Thorogood, what Terry and I will have to live on? You will realise it is a matter of some urgency to us both."

"Yes, of course, Miss Orlena," Mr. Thorogood replied. "I think at a conservative estimate you will each find yourselves in possession of something in the proximity of two hundred thousand pounds!"

As the Solicitor's voice died away there was a dead silence and the two young people facing him appeared to be turned to stone.

Their eyes were on his face and Mr. Thorogood was actor enough to appreciate the sensation he had caused.

"D-did you . . . say . . . two *hundred* thousand . . . pounds?" Orlena asked in a voice that sounded strangled.

"I did, Miss Orlena, and it is with great pleasure that I can impart this news, which I know must be very welcome both to you and to Sir Terence."

"Good God!" Terry ejaculated, having apparently found his voice.

After a moment, as no-one spoke, he said:

"Do you mean to say that our father was sitting on all that money and refusing to give us a penny?"

He rose to his feet to stand at the desk towering over Mr. Thorogood as he said:

"Do you realise I have had to go without decent clothes? To go on my knees to the local farmers to beg for a ride on one of their horses? That he refused to let me go to London after I left Oxford, and whatever I asked for the answer was always the same: 'We have no money—I cannot afford it!'"

Terry's voice was raised in such an unrestrained way that Mr. Thorogood couched reproachfully before he said:

"It would be most unseemly, Sir Terence, to speak ill of the dead, but I think between these four walls we can admit that your father, the late Sir Hamish, was in fact a miser."

"How could we have imagined—how could we have dreamt for a moment that he was not as poor as he said he was?" Terry asked in bewilderment.

He looked at his sister as he spoke and as Orlena's grey eyes met his she said hardly above a whisper:

"He . . . refused to let Mama go . . . abroad when she was so . . . ill. The doctors said that . . . if she went to the sun when it was so cold here she . . . might live."

There was a throb in her voice which showed she was not far from tears and her brother moved towards her to put his arm round her.

"I know what you are feeling," he said, "but it is no use looking back into the past. Now we can look forward to the future—a very different future, Orlena, from what we had visualised."

"There is something further I have to tell you," Mr. Thorogood interposed.

The two young people turned their faces towards him.

"The money is rightfully yours," Mr. Thorogood

continued, "but you do not have the handling of it until you reach the age of twenty-one."

"That is in three months' time," Terry said, "so I will not have long to wait!"

"Until you both attain your majority," Mr. Thorogood went on as if he had not spoken, "your father appointed a Guardian to control your wealth."

"A Guardian?" Terry exclaimed in astonishment. "Who is it?"

Mr. Thorogood slowly drew some other papers from his brief-case.

"This deed," he said, "was executed three years ago after your mother passed away. If your father had died before Lady Weldon, she would of course have been your legal Guardian."

"We realise that," Terry said, "but who did our father appoint?"

"His friend the Earl of Ulverston," Mr. Thorogood answered.

"Ulverston?" Terry exclaimed. "Who the devil is he?"

He looked at Orlena as he spoke and after a moment she said:

"He was a friend of Papa's for many years. They were at Oxford together, and I think they used to communicate occasionally, but I have not heard him speak of the Earl for a long time."

She looked at her brother as she spoke, and they both knew that after their mother's death their father had in fact become to all intents and purposes a little mad.

He had shut himself away from all his friends and acquaintances and grown meaner month by month, year by year, refusing to spend a penny-piece if he could possibly help it, until they had really believed that they were as poor as he pretended to be.

Orlena thought now it was only by a miracle that Terry had been allowed to finish his time at Oxford, she had come off worst.

Her father had not allowed her to continue her education and had dismissed the Governess whom her mother had chosen for her. He also refused to employ the teachers and Professors who had previously come to Weldon Park to instruct her.

He had sold the horses, with the exception of those that were too old to fetch any price except from the Knacker's Yard, and dismissed the servants.

They had been served by a few very old retainers who shuffled round the house and grounds doing as little as possible and were too ancient to find other employment.

Their wages had been cut to a minimum and they had barely existed on the small amount of food that Sir Hamish allowed to be purchased.

It all seemed now, Orlena thought a nightmare, and to know there had been no reason for it and that her mother might in fact have lived if she had been given the treatment which the doctors prescribed was almost too hard to bear.

Her thoughts returned to the present as she heard Terry say:

"Will this Guardian of ours interfere? How can we get in touch with him?"

"I have already written to His Lordship," Mr. Thorogood replied, "to acquaint him with the news of your father's death and to inform him of his duties towards you both."

"Where does he live?"

"In London. I think it would be polite—and perhaps expedient—for you both to visit him as soon as it is possible for you to do so."

"London!" Terry's eyes lit up. "You are suggesting we should go to London?"

"I am sure, Sir Terence, that you could not expect the Earl, who is an elderly gentleman, to come here."

"No, of course not!" Terry agreed quickly. "Orlena and I would be only too delighted to visit him in London, would we not, Orlena?"

He smiled at his sister as he spoke and she saw the excitement in his face.

She knew, as she had known before, how bitterly he had resented not being able to go to London as most of his friends from Oxford had done.

He had wanted to join the Bucks and Dandies who were to be found in the brilliant society which centred round the Prince of Wales.

She had no such aspirations.

When she was eighteen and had realised that her mother's plan that she should make her curtsey at Buckingham Palace and make her début during the Season had no chance of materialising, she had resigned herself to living quietly and frugally at home.

The following year had passed by with nothing more eventful than Terry's return from Oxford.

That he had been resentful and disagreeable had not lessened her pleasure at his presence.

Because Orlena loved her brother he had brought an interest and an excitement into her life which made her never for a moment regret that she could not enjoy the company of her contemporaries.

"London, Orlena!" Terry said again. "We will go there at once!"

He looked at Mr. Thorogood with a question in his eyes.

"I have already discussed this matter with my partners," Mr. Thorogood said, "and we are prepared to advance you, Sir Terence and Miss Orlena, the sum of one hundred pounds to cover your travelling expenses."

"One hundred pounds! That will certainly be better than nothing!" Terry exclaimed. "For I can assure you, Mr. Thorogood, that my pockets are completely 'to let'!"

"Thank you. It is very kind of you," Orlena said.

"Of course, when you arrive in London," Mr. Thorogood continued, "I am confident you will find that His Lordship will make you a proper allowance, so that you can purchase clothes and anything else you require. He will also doubtless see that Miss Orlena is provided with a Chaperon."

"A Chaperon?" Terry exclaimed. "What in the world does Orlena want with a Chaperon?"

"You seem to forget, Sir Terence, that your sister is, if I may say so, a very attractive young woman. It would be extremely improper for her to live alone without the companionship of a lady who has reached the years of discretion."

Terry continued to look astonished at the idea, and Mr. Thorogood went on:

"I dare say it will not be long before Miss Orlena is married, and you yourself, Sir Terence, might bring home a bride. In the meantime, I am quite certain you can rely on the Earl of Ulverston to assist you in every way possible and advise you as to the spending of your very considerable fortune."

"I need no advice on that," Terry replied impulsively. "I want horses, Mr. Thorogood, horses that are not like those tumbledown nags I have had to ride, horses that can gallop and jump. And when I do return, I promise you I shall join every hunt in the neighbourhood."

"I hope you will, Sir Terence, and I assure you it will please everyone if you should open Weldon Park and make it like it was in your grandfather's day and when your father and mother first married."

"I have every intention of putting my house in order," Terry said.

Now there was a more serious note in his voice, and a touch of resolution in his tone which made Orlena smile at him with a deep affection.

Terry would do the right thing, she was sure of that. At the same time, she knew how much he had resented having nothing to do, nothing to spend, and most of all nothing to ride.

How could her father, she asked herself, have been so cruel as to let Terry suffer as he had suffered since he had returned from Oxford the previous summer?

Granted, he had only to kick his heels for months, while she had done it for years.

But it had been long enough for her to realise that a man should have his time fully occupied, and that was something her father had deliberately prevented Terry from experiencing.

"We will leave for London tomorrow or the next day," Terry said now in a firm voice. "The sooner we see our Guardian, the better!"

A sudden thought struck him and he turned towards the Solicitor.

"I suppose he cannot prevent us from having the money my father left us?"

"A Guardian's duty is to prevent you from dissipating the capital of your fortune," Mr. Thorogood replied pompously, "and to decide how much of the income you should receive yearly until you reach your majority."

"He has only three months in which to execute his jurisdiction over me," Terry reflected.

"I am quite certain you will find His Lordship will be extremely generous," Mr. Thorogood affirmed. "There is no reason for him to act otherwise."

"No, of course not," Terry said in a relieved voice.

Orlena knew he was worrying over details because it was as difficult for him as it was for her to realise the magnitude of the wealth their father had left them.

Looking back, she thought it would have been impossible for them to suspect that he was not speaking the truth about their penury.

He had been furiously angry over any so-called extravagance, and finally, just before he died, he had resented any expenditure, however small.

Memories of the rows there had been over the tradesmen's bills made her say to Mr. Thorogood:

"There are, I think, a few outstanding debts."

"I will deal with all those, Miss Orlena," he replied.

"And would it be possible to take on a few more servants?" Orlena asked. "The place needs a great deal of cleaning, since it has been too much for those we employ. After all, the house is very big and it was impossible for them to do everything that Papa expected them to do."

"I am well aware of that, Miss Orlena," Mr. Thorogood smiled. "If you will permit me to pay off what debts are outstanding and increase the staff both inside and outside the house, I think the other matters can wait until you have seen the Earl of Ulverston."

He paused and added:

"Either you can write to me from London or His Lordship can instruct me to take what steps are necessary before your return."

"Thank you very much," Orlena said.

"Before you start talking about our return," Terry interposed, "let us make plans for our departure—that is what is important!"

"I expect, Sir Terence, you will wish to travel by Post-Chaise," Mr. Thorogood said. "I am returning immediately to York and if I can be of any assistance in speaking to the Posting-Inn in North Street, I am only too willing to stop there on my way."

"Post-Chaise!" Terry exclaimed. "Wait a minute! I have an idea!"

He walked towards the door.

"I will tell you about it later, Orlena, but I think we will enjoy our drive more if I tool my own horses."

He left the Library, slamming the door behind him, and they heard his footsteps running across the uncarpeted Hall.

Orlena turned to Mr. Thorogood with a smile.

"I do not know what Terry has in mind," she

said, "but I must thank you for making us both very happy."

"It is one of the most pleasant tasks I have ever undertaken, Miss Orlena," Mr. Thorogood replied. "I am well aware how difficult things have been both for you and for your brother these past years."

He gave a deep sigh.

"But you will understand," he continued, "that although I was aware to some extent of your father's fortune, it was a confidential matter and my lips were sealed."

"Of course, Mr. Thorogood, I understand," Orlena answered.

"I tried to speak to your father on more than one occasion, but he was determined to brook no interference from me or from anybody else."

"I know what Papa was like."

Her voice was grave as she went on:

"It has been difficult . . . very difficult, Mr. Thorogood, but now it is all over and Terry will be able to enjoy himself as he has always longed to do."

"And so will you, Miss Orlena," Mr. Thorogood said gently.

"I . . . suppose so," Orlena replied doubtfully, "but I have grown used to living here very . . . quietly."

She was about to say more, but she stopped herself.

She felt that the Lawyer would not understand if she told him that in some strange way she was almost frightened of the world outside Weldon Park.

She had been nearly sixteen when her mother died, and for the last three years she had seen practically no-one but her father and the old servants.

Terry had not even come home from Oxford in the vacations. There had always been friends who had asked him to stay in their country Estates.

When she did see him, he talked only of the

horses he had ridden, the parties he had been to, and people of whom she had never heard and with whom she felt she would have very little in common.

It was in fact very frightening, she told herself later when Mr. Thorogood had gone and she was alone, to think of leaving her home and going into a strange world of which she had no knowledge, and where she had no friends.

Then she told herself she must do as Terry wanted.

He was the one who really mattered, and until he married, which she was sure would not be for a long time, she would have to act as hostess for him at Weldon Park or anywhere else they lived.

Terry did not return to the house for some hours and Orlena took the opportunity of going to the kitchen and telling old Mrs. Burrows, the Cook, that they could have a very different dinner from the one she had planned.

"Sir Terence and I are going to London, Mrs. Burrows," Orlena told her, "and when we return you shall either have kitchen-maids to help you, or else if you wish you and your husband can retire to one of the cottages on the Estate."

She saw the astonishment in the old woman's face and went on:

"I know they are in a bad state of repair, but now there will be money to do them up and I promise you that Sir Terence and I will see that you are comfortable."

"Be this true what you're a-telling me, Miss Orlena?" Mrs. Burrows enquired.

"It is indeed!" Orlena replied. "Papa had money of which we had no knowledge, and now we can spend it on restoring the house and having plenty of staff like there used to be in the old days."

She put her hand on Mrs. Burrows's arm and added:

"Mr. Thorogood will see to everything while we are away and he has promised to increase your wages immediately."

Mrs. Burrows wiped her eyes.

"It's a shock to me, Miss, I don't mind telling you. After all the skimping and saving we've done, you tells me the master had money!"

"We have certainly skimped and saved," Orlena agreed, "but now it is over and the best thing we can do is not even think about it."

But even as she spoke she knew she would never forget how her mother had not been allowed to go abroad, how her father had kept repeating over and over again that it was quite impossible for him to find the money to send her to a warmer climate.

"And yet Papa loved her!" Orlena said to herself in bewilderment.

She thought it over and came to the conclusion that perhaps it was not only meanness on his part that had made him sacrifice his wife's health, but was also his dislike at the thought of leaving home.

'Like me, he did not wish to face the world outside,' Orlena thought.

Then, afraid that she might have grown like her father, she told herself she had to be sensible.

At her age it was ridiculous to think of incarcerating herself in any house, however fond of it she might be, and of course she needed new gowns.

When she reached London she was quite certain she would enjoy meeting young people of her own age, even though the idea of it made her feel a little nervous.

She looked at herself in the mirror and wondered if anyone would notice her in London.

There was no doubt that Terry would be a success.

He was not only tall, handsome, well dressed, and extremely elegant, he also had a self-confidence which carried him through awkward situations with flying colours and made him popular with everyone he met.

Orlena looked at her reflection again.

It was difficult to visualise what she would look like if she was dressed in the new fashionably slim and elegant gowns of muslin and gauze; if she wore on her head a high-crowned bonnet trimmed with satin ribbons and feathers.

The only clothes she possessed she had either grown out of, so that they were almost indecently tight, or they had belonged to her mother.

They were therefore full-skirted and tight-waisted with fichus over the shoulders.

"I shall look a regular dowdy if I appear in London like this," Orlena told herself with a flash of humour.

Then she thought that, if she did, it would bring home to the Earl even more forcibly that she must have a very large allowance with which to purchase a new wardrobe.

She thought of Mr. Thorogood's suggestion of a Chaperon and felt a little nervous.

The Earl's idea and hers might be very different, and the thought of some bossy domineering woman ordering her about made Orlena feel apprehensive.

Then she thought she was just frightening herself with childish "bogeys" which had no substance and were merely a part of her imagination.

She was quite certain that once they met the Earl of Ulverston, his one idea would be to settle their affairs as quickly as possible and with the least trouble and obligation to himself.

'Terry and I will rent a house where we can live comfortably on our income,' Orlena planned.

Then suddenly a thought came to her that made her eyes shine.

In London she would be able to visit the Opera

and concerts, and to obtain all the books she wanted to read.

It was a thought that excited her far more than the prospect of Balls, Assemblies, or Receptions.

She had felt starved of something far more important to her than food ever since her father had dismissed her Governess and stopped her music lessons.

"If you want education you can teach yourself," he had said.

At the same time, he had refused to take the daily newspapers or allow her to buy books.

There were quite a number in the house, but they had been bought for the Library by her grandfather and even the newest of them was twenty-five years out of date.

Nevertheless, she had made the best of a situation which she could not alter.

Sometimes she saw copies of the *Ladies' Journal* which belonged to the Vicar's wife. These kept her up to date with the fashions and told her some of the things that were happening in other parts of the world.

The Vicar would lend her books on subjects which interested him, although unfortunately they seldom coincided with her own.

There was nothing she could do about her music except to play the piano. Because she could not afford to buy the works of famous composers, she herself composed.

She put all her thoughts, her beliefs, and her dreams into the melodies she played in the big, cold Salon.

She played and read, and this helped to make time pass if not quickly at least comparatively pleasantly until Terry returned home.

Then everything changed.

He insisted on buying the newspapers, even

though he had to pay for them out of the few shillings which were all he had to bless himself with.

He told her about his friends and their houses and the race-meetings he had attended with them; the Mills he had watched; the Balls at which he had undoubtedly been a success with the girls he had partnered.

It was all fascinating and Orlena had sat like a child listening to a fairy-story while Terry had been content to have her as an audience.

"It is a damned shame that you cannot make yourself look decent and at least get invited to the Balls which take place at York," he had said once.

Orlena had laughed.

"I really would look like the beggar-maid at the feast! And even if I received and accepted such an invitation, how do you think I would get there? You know Papa would never let me hire a carriage, and I am sure the horses we have now in the stables would never make the journey to York and back."

That was true, as Terry knew, and only to mention horses was to bring a scowl between his eyes and a squaring of his chin, which made Orlena avoid the subject whenever possible.

But this evening he had returned just before dinner and when she heard him shouting to her from the Hall she ran down the stairs, knowing before she reached him that he had something exciting to impart.

"I have done it, Orlena! I have done it!" he said.

"Done what?" she enquired, almost breathless from the speed at which she had run.

"I have borrowed a curricle in which I can drive you to London."

"You have?"

"You remember old Farmer Denby's son—the one who spent so much money that everyone was suspicious and finally was arrested because he had got in with a gang of forgers?"

"Yes, of course I remember," Orlena replied. "It was a scandal in the neighbourhood for at least a year."

"Well, I remembered that just before he was caught and transported he had been driving a curricle," Terry said. "It is a bit out of date now and there are later and more-fashionable models, but it will carry us to London. The very first thing I will buy is a really slap-up turn-out that you will not be ashamed to travel in."

"I would not be ashamed anyway," Orlena laughed. "But how clever of you, Terry, to have remembered it."

"I was quite prepared to buy it from Farmer Denby, but when I told him that both you and I had been left a fortune by Papa and are going to make the place like it was in the old days, he was only too glad to co-operate. So he has loaned me the curricle—it is no use to him anyway."

"That is exciting!" Orlena said. "But what about horses?"

"I am not going to buy any old nags that are offered to me," Terry said loftily. "I am not as green as that. I am going to wait until I get to London. I shall go to Tattersall's and take my time in setting up a stable of my own."

"I am sure that is wise," Orlena remarked.

"There are always crooks ready to sell a greenhorn from the country showy beasts without any stamina in them."

"You will be much too clever for them," Orlena said admiringly.

"I intend to be," Terry replied, "but it means, Orlena, that we shall have to travel with post-horses."

"That does not worry me."

"It is not what I would wish," Terry said. "We can afford, you and I, to do things in style in the future, and that is what we will do. But it is no use wasting time and money on a lot of rubbish. You agree to that?"

"Yes, of course."

"Very well, we will do things the sensible way," Terry said. "We will go to London just as we are, and the quicker the better. Then we will buy everything of the best—the best horses, the best vehicles, and the finest clothes that Savile Row for me and Bond Street for you can provide."

He spoke with so much excitement in his voice that Orlena clapped her hands.

"Oh, Terry, you make it sound such an adventure!"

"That is exactly what it is going to be," he said, "and although I have been cursing Papa for what he has made us suffer these past years, I suppose really we should bless him. After all, he might have spent the money on himself!"

"Yes, of . . . course," Orlena agreed.

There was just a little hesitation before she spoke, as she thought again of her mother.

Then she told herself that the one thing she must not do was dampen Terry's enthusiasm or spoil in any way the happiness of what lay ahead.

"The past is past," she told herself.

Then because when she was alone she was used to talking to her mother she said in her heart:

'Please, darling Mama, help us. I have a feeling we shall both need your help.'

* * *

The curricle in which they set off two mornings later from Weldon Park was in fact not as impressive as Orlena had expected.

Although it had been washed down and polished, the two years it had stood in Farmer Denby's barn, covered with the dust of straw and hay and used as a perch by innumerable chickens, had not improved the paintwork.

There was also definitely quite a lot of rust which no amount of polishing would remove.

But at least it was comfortable, and even though

the leather seats were torn in several places Terry assured Orlena that if it rained the hood would prove quite adequate to protect them both from the elements.

Orlena hoped this was true because it was inevitable that there would be showers in April, and although she had brought her thick cloak with her she had no wish to be soaked to the skin and arrive in London with a streaming cold.

They each had so little to pack that everything they possessed was accommodated under the seat and in one trunk, which was strapped on the back of the vehicle.

The two horses which had come from the nearest Posting-House were not a pair nor were they very much to look at, but they started off at a good pace and travelled a reasonable number of miles on the first day.

There had been much to do before leaving and in her excitement she had found it difficult to sleep, so that Orlena was extremely tired the first night of their journey.

Despite the fact that her bed in the Inn at which they stopped was hard and the window let in a considerable amount of cold wind, she slept peacefully.

They set off the next morning with a fresh pair of horses and once again they had no mishaps and reached the town where they were to stay the night within an hour of the time planned.

It was on the third day that Terry began to complain.

He had insisted that they should leave very early in the morning, and Orlena, being used to waking early, was punctual and usually ready before he was.

"I think this is a damned dull road," Terry grumbled. "If you ask me, it is very monotonous just driving, driving, without a break."

"What do you want to do?" Orlena asked.

She had a feeling that there was some special

reason behind what he was saying, for up until now
he had been only too thrilled to drive the horses,
even though they were not of the best quality.

For a moment Terry looked almost sheepish, then
he said:

"I have learnt that there are races today at Newmarket."

There was a pause, then as Orlena did not speak
he continued:

"We shall get there before noon."

"Are you telling me you want to attend the
races?" Orlena enquired.

"Why not?" Terry asked. "I have always wanted
to go to Newmarket. In fact, one of my friends at Oxford asked me to stay with him for the autumn meeting, but his father wanted to take him to Scotland
so he had to put me off."

"Perhaps we could see the races today," Orlena
said, knowing that that was what Terry wanted her to
say.

"Do you mean that?" he asked. "You would not
mind?"

"I would love it if it amused you," Orlena replied. "I have never seen a big race-meeting. I remember going to the York races when I was thirteen and
I enjoyed it enormously."

"I tell you what we will do," Terry said, who had
obviously not been listening to anything she said. "We
will stay the night at Newmarket. Why not? We have
enough money."

"Are you quite . . . sure?" Orlena asked nervously.

"I am quite sure," he answered. "Leave everything
to me, Orlena. We will watch the races, find somewhere to stay, and set off for London next morning.
I made enquiries last night and they say that as the
roads are so much better than they were it should
only take us about six hours."

He flicked the horses with his whip as if to hurry them, as he continued:

"If we leave early, say about eight o'clock, we should reach Ulverston House soon after luncheon. I do not suppose His Lordship would wish to see us before that."

"No, of course not," Orlena agreed.

She could not help feeling nervous at the thought of meeting Lord Ulverston, but she told herself there was no good reason for it. After all, he would be about the same age as their father, who had only been sixty-six when he died.

Following her train of thought, she said:

"I cannot help feeling that Papa would have lived to be very much older if he had taken more care of himself last winter. You know how he refused to buy coal and the wood fires were not enough to keep the house warm. What was more, he would not have one in his bed-room."

Terry took one hand from the reins and laid it on hers as she sat beside him.

"Forget it," he said, "and if we are honest, we should both be grateful he did not live any longer. I know now he must have been mad as a coot before he died, and getting worse. God knows what would have happened next year, judging from the way he behaved this year!"

He made a sound of sheer relief and cried:

"We are free of him, Orlena! We are like birds which have been let out of a cage. For goodness' sake, let us enjoy ourselves!"

"Yes . . . of course," Orlena agreed. "It was silly of me to mention it."

"We are going to stay at Newmarket," Terry said firmly. "You shall see for yourself the smart people who attend race-meetings, and you will see the horses —magnificent horses, Orlena! Just like those I am going to own—and race!"

"Terry!" Orlena exclaimed.

This was an ambition of which she had not heard previously.

"Of course I am going to race my own horses," Terry said, "and when they bring home the big prizes you will be proud of me!"

"I shall always be that," Orlena said quietly.

He smiled at her and as they journeyed on she felt she had never been so happy.

There was a closeness between herself and her brother that was more pronounced than it had ever been before, and they were setting off together on a great adventure.

'I must do everything Terry wants,' Orlena thought.

They reached Newmarket, which was crowded with people and vehicles, and stopped at the largest, best-looking Inn in the small town.

Outside there were a great number of coaches, calashes, Phaetons, and curricles, attended by smartly liveried servants with cockaded hats and shining crested buttons.

"It looks very grand!" Orlena said in a low voice. "I am sure they will be full up and not have accommodation for us."

"I will go and find out," Terry said determinedly. "Hold the reins for me."

He handed them to Orlena as he spoke, then stepped from the curricle and walked towards the entrance to the Inn.

Orlena realised she need not worry about restraining the horses, which seemed already tired, although they had been going for only a few hours.

They were not nearly so spirited as those they had hired previously and she thought that, considering the money they had paid for them, they had been overcharged.

She had not to wait long before Terry reappeared and she knew by one glance at his face that she had been right in thinking all the accommodation was taken.

"I am afraid, dearest," she said as he climbed into the curricle beside her, "that when the races take place, every room in the town will have been engaged for a long time."

"I am not giving in so easily," Terry replied. "We will try the Lamb. It looks quite a decent sort of place."

But the Lamb was full and they moved on down the road, looking for another Inn, with Orlena feeling despondently that Terry was bound to be disappointed.

They stopped outside a very ancient-looking hostelry called the Bushel. The façade had two pillars supporting large bay windows on the first floor and looked rather attractive.

There were not so many vehicles outside it, and as Terry handed her the reins for the third time Orlena hoped that he would be lucky.

She had the feeling that the Bushel was the last Inn in Newmarket, and if he failed here there would be nothing for it but to travel on towards London.

Inside there were low ceilings and a number of well-dressed staff moving round, and Terry looked for someone who might be in charge.

He found the Inn-keeper, a fat, middle-aged man with his shirt-sleeves up, wearing a white apron.

He was scolding a potman for not having the glasses properly polished, but his voice trailed off when Terry appeared to enquire politely:

"Can I do anything to serve you, Sir?"

"My name is Sir Terence Weldon," Terry replied in a manner which he knew was impressive. "My sister and I are on our way to London and we require two rooms for the night."

The Inn-keeper shook his head.

"Being race-week . . ." he began, then he stopped. "Wait a minute, Sir, I think I might be able to help you."

He crossed the floor and opening a door shouted:

"Did you tell me, Moll, that th' Duke was not a-coming back?"

From somewhere in the bowels of the Inn a voice floated back:

"No, 'e be leavin' after th' races. Oi've cleaned 'is rooms."

The Inn-keeper returned to Terry.

"You're in luck, Sir. His Grace th' Duke of Northaw has just vacated our two best bed-chambers and a private Sitting-Room."

"I will take them!" Terry said quickly.

"They'll be eight guineas for the night, Sir."

Terry was well aware that this was an exorbitant charge, but he realised that at the time of the races the Hoteliers could ask anything they wished. As Newmarket was in a somewhat isolated part of the country, there was no question of their not being able to fill their Inns.

"That will be all right," Terry replied. "Send a porter for the baggage and your ostler can take the horses round to the stable."

"Very good, Sir."

Terry walked outside smiling and before he spoke Orlena knew that he had been successful.

"Two Ducal bed-rooms and a private Sitting-Room," he told her. "What more could anyone ask?"

"It sounds very expensive!"

"Very!" he replied. "But why should that worry us? Hurry up! We will have something to eat, then we will go to the race-course."

"That will be exciting!" Orlena smiled.

She climbed out of the curricle and hurried into the Inn.

A mob-capped maid met her and showed her the way upstairs to a delightful room with a beamed ceiling and a four-poster bed which had, she was assured, a most comfortable mattress made of goosefeathers.

When the luggage had been brought upstairs, Orlena went down to be shown into a private room where Terry was waiting for her.

"Luncheon will be served in a few minutes, Sir," the Inn-keeper informed them.

Orlena waited until the door closed behind him, and as her eyes met her brother's they both began to laugh.

She ran towards him and he pulled her close against him.

"It is fun, is it not, Orlena?" he said, his eyes alight with excitement.

"It is wonderful . . . marvellous," Orlena replied. "But I am sure I am dreaming and we will both wake up!"

Chapter Two

After a rest the horses set off at a brisk pace and Orlena felt excited at the thought of seeing the races.

It was a warm day for April and instead of the bitter winds which she had heard often swept over the Heath there was a fitful sunshine that brought exquisite lights to the land undulating away towards the distant horizon.

She had discarded her cloak and was wearing a deep-blue travelling-gown which her mother had worn for several years and which Orlena knew was sadly out of fashion.

Nevertheless it became her and she only wished that her bonnet was more in vogue.

But she had pressed the satin ribbons, already shining from frequent ironings, and their colour threw into prominence the transparent quality of her skin.

Knowing few men except her brother, she had no idea that she looked very lovely and in some ways unlike any other girl of her age, as with her eyes shining and her hands clasped together with excitement she sat beside Terry in the curricle.

They arrived at the Heath and saw that, although the races had not yet started, along the course there were rows of carriages three or four deep, most of them standing without their horses.

At the betting-post there was a huge crowd of livery-servants, the lowest sharpers and black legs, grooms, gentlemen, and doubtless rogues all placing their money.

Terry looking round drove his horses to the top of a rise, where there were only a few smart Phaetons and elegant curricles lined up.

"We can see splendidly from here," Orlena exclaimed.

Terry looked round him.

"I can see the horses being paraded," he said. "Do you wish to come and look at them?"

"Yes, of course," Orlena said, "but how can we leave our own pair?"

Terry beckoned to a ragged boy who was wandering round, obviously in the hope of earning a penny or two.

"Hi, boy!" he called. "Come and look after my horses!"

"Oi'll do that, Guv'nor," the boy said eagerly.

"I suppose I can trust you," Terry said.

"Oi won't lollop off wiv'em, if that's what ye fink, Guv'."

"You had better not!" Terry warned.

He helped Orlena from the curricle and they set off down the hill.

Never had Orlena thought she would see such magnificent horse-flesh at close quarters.

They all seemed to be what Terry called "in the pink of condition," and their jockeys in their brilliant coats and caps made the parade very colourful.

Terry talked to several of the men standing round and Orlena saw him take some sovereigns from his pocket.

"You are not betting, Terry, are you?" she asked a little nervously as they walked back again towards their curricle.

"Only a trifle," Terry admitted. "One can hardly come to a race-meeting without backing one's fancy."

"I hope you win!" Orlena said beneath her breath.

She was thinking how horrified her father would be if he knew. Then she told herself that Terry was right, the past was past and now he could well afford to have a bet.

They got back into the curricle, Terry rewarding the small boy who had looked after it, and watched the horses lining up for the start.

"What are the colours of the one you have backed?" Orlena asked.

Suddenly, before Terry could reply, there was the noise of galloping hoofs behind them and they both turned their heads.

Coming towards them down the Heath was a magnificent team of chestnuts moving at what appeared to be an outrageous pace.

As Orlena stared she saw that the team was being driven by the smartest and in a way the most fantastic gentleman she had ever seen in her life.

She knew he was driving superbly, but it was in fact his whole appearance which made her unable to stop looking at him.

He was wearing a driving-coat with no less than fifteen capes, which she knew denoted that he was a Corinthian.

His high hat was set at a raffish angle on his dark head, while an exquisitely tied white cravat framed his square chin.

She did not know how she managed to take in every detail of his appearance, but as he drew nearer and still nearer she saw that he was in fact exceedingly handsome.

As she watched, almost mesmerised by the speed at which he was driving, he drew his team suddenly to a standstill almost directly behind their own curricle.

Then his eyes, dark, hard, and penetrating, seemed to take in their position and with an expression of obvious contempt he said:

"Out of my way!"

The words were drawled and yet unmistakably clear and commanding.

Terry stiffened.

For a moment he could not believe they were addressed to him. Then as he realised that the hard eyes of the Corinthian were looking directly at him he replied defensively:

"I was here first!"

Without turning his head, still in the lazy drawl which managed to be offensive and at the same time authoritative, the gentleman said:

"Move them, Jason!"

For a moment Orlena could not think to whom he spoke, when from behind the Phaeton a groom jumped to the ground.

He was almost as elegantly dressed as his master. His cockaded hat was worn at the same angle, his liveried coat with its crested buttons fitted him like a glove.

He walked to the front of the curricle, seized the two horses by their bridles, and started to turn their heads.

"What the devil do you think you are doing?" Terry asked angrily.

The groom did not reply and again the lazy voice from the Phaeton behind them spoke.

"Tell them, Jason!"

"This 'ere place be reserved fo' members of th' Jockey Club," the groom said. "There be plenty of th' rest o' th' Heath left for turnip-tops."

Orlena felt herself blush.

She was well aware that members of the Jockey Club were specially privileged persons on any race-course, and she thought too late that Terry should have enquired on their arrival whether they were infringing any rule or usurping any privileges.

The groom relentlessly turned the horses and led them out of the place they had occupied.

There was nothing Terry could do but grit his teeth and hold the reins until the groom had released the bridles.

Only as the space they had occupied was cleared did Orlena look back to see the Corinthian moving his team into it, smoothly and with an expertise which she knew any driver would have envied.

Whipping up his horses, Terry drove away muttering angrily beneath his breath.

"How the hell was I to know it was reserved for the Jockey Club?" he asked as they moved along the rise.

"You could not have known, and it would not have hurt the gentleman to have told us more politely," Orlena replied.

"Did you see his horses?" Terry asked. "I will damn well have their equal—or better—if it is the last thing I do!"

Orlena could not help thinking it was unlikely that any man, even Terry, good-looking though he was, could ever emulate that air of consequence—almost insolence—of the Corinthian.

But as she had no right to spoil her brother's day she did everything she could to smooth his ruffled feelings.

Soon, having found another place from which they could watch, they were both too entranced by the races to think any more of the unpleasantness that had occurred before they had started.

Suddenly there would be the cry "The horses have started!" and all the betters would rush to the edges of the course. Every carriage was filled with persons levelling telescopes and opera-glasses.

A manager on horseback kept the course clear, applying his whip to the shoulders of any intruder.

Then after a momentary silence there was a wild uproar, shouts, curses, and cheers re-echoing on every side, as the horses swept past the post.

To Orlena it was an excitement she had never

imagined and she understood why Terry wished to race his own horses.

They returned to the Bushel after the last race was over, and having dropped Orlena at the front door Terry took the curricle round to the stable.

Now that she was not in such a hurry she had time to notice the racing prints hung round the big open fireplace, and taking a quick glance in what was obviously the Bar she saw dozens of bottles ready, as if the Hotel was expecting a great deal of custom once the racing was over.

She went upstairs to her bed-room and as the maid helped her change her gown she told Orlena many things she wished to know, all of which she was ready to relate to her brother when she met him downstairs in their private Sitting-Room.

He too had changed for dinner, and she thought he looked very elegant in the evening-clothes he had worn at Oxford.

Only she knew that all his cravats were frayed at the edges and his shirts desperately in need of being replaced.

"I have found out such exciting things!" she told him after they had ordered dinner and sat down to wait for it in front of the log fire.

"What sort of things?" Terry enquired.

"That this is the oldest Inn in the town, and Charles II used to stay here."

"It certainly looks old enough to have accommodated him," Terry remarked, glancing at the heavy beamed ceiling and the panelling of the room, which was dark with age.

"There is his cock-pit in the cellar," Orlena went on.

Terry looked more interested.

"I wonder if there is a chance of a fight tonight."

"I hope not," Orlena said quickly. "I think it is a horrid, cruel sport!"

"It is certainly not a sight for women," Terry replied, "but there is no need for you to worry your head about it—you can go to bed, Orlena."

"There is something even more exciting," Orlena said, trying to take his mind off the cock-fighting. "There is a tunnel down in the cellar which leads to a house which was once Nell Gwynn's."

Terry was not interested in this and she wished she had not mentioned the cock-fighting, for he was obviously thinking about it.

She tried to get him interested in the fact that Queen Anne had been a patron of Newmarket races and to discuss with him the famous scandal involving the jockey Sam Chifney.

This had taken place twelve years ago, in 1791, when he was riding Escape, a horse which belonged to the Prince of Wales.

But she realised that Terry was not really listening to her, and after a time she lapsed into silence.

The dinner when it came was delicious and because they were both hungry they ate quickly. As soon as they had finished Terry rose from the table.

"I am going to look round and see what is happening," he said. "It sounds as if things are warming up."

Orlena had been aware for some time that there was the sound of loud voices and bursts of laughter coming from the other parts of the Inn, and she thought how happy everyone sounded and that it must have been a very successful meeting.

She realised however that Terry had not told her whether he had won or lost. She naturally suspected the worst.

"Go to bed, Orlena," her brother said now. "We ought to leave sharp at eight o'clock, so we had best breakfast in here soon after seven."

"I will not be late," Orlena promised. "Thank you, Terry, for taking me to the races. It was very interesting."

"The next time I bring you, we will come in style," he smiled.

Then, eager to be gone, he left the private Sitting-Room and Orlena was alone.

She sat for a little while looking into the fire, then she thought Terry was right and she had best go to bed.

The noise and laughter had increased and seemed almost deafening when the waiters opened the door to clear away their dinner and she could not help feeling that men had much more fun than women.

She was quite sure that Terry would soon make friends with the other gentlemen patronising the Bushel, and perhaps he would find as he hoped that a cock-fight was taking place.

Even while she hated the idea of it, she could understand that it was one of the sports in which most gambling men were interested.

It seemed rather hot in the small Sitting-Room and she pulled back the curtains to open the window and found that she was looking out onto a garden at the back of the Inn.

She unfastened a diamond-paned casement and there was the fragrance of jasmine, and in the light streaming out from the uncurtained windows she could see daffodils in a golden profusion under fruit trees which were in blossom.

Everything was much more forward than it had been in the North and Orlena suddenly had a longing to see the flowers closer and smell their scent.

They had eaten their luncheon so hastily that she had not noticed the garden until now.

She was wearing a warm dinner-gown of sapphire-blue velvet which was in fact the best she had. It was almost threadbare, for both she and her mother had worn it for many years.

But Orlena had arranged a fresh white fichu

round the neck, and although the skirt was full and
out-of-date it became her and made her look very
young and very lovely.

"I will not be cold," she told herself. "Anyway,
I will only be in the garden for a short time."

She opened the door of the Sitting-Room and
heard coming from the Bar a burst of laughter which
seemed almost to shake the ceilings.

Then she found, as she had hoped, a door not
far from where she was standing which obviously
opened onto the garden.

She moved towards it, certain that everybody
would be too busy to notice her, and a moment or so
later found herself outside.

There was no wind, the air was mellow, and, as
she had expected, the fragrance of the flowers and
shrubs was enchanting.

She smelt lilac and found a huge bush of purple
blossoms beside a smaller one which was white.

It was quite easy to see her way by the light
from the windows of the Inn and she moved further
and further down the garden until she found a small
water-lily pond and beside it a rough wooden seat.

She sat down and felt the beauty and the fragrance of it all bring a new melody into her conscious-
ness.

As always when she composed her tunes, they
would suddenly seem to ring in her ears and repeat
themselves over and over again until she knew that
if she was at the piano she could play them.

'I wonder if many people have written a tune at
Newmarket?' she thought whimsically.

She was sure that the rollicking Courtiers who
had surrounded Charles II had written odes to the
ladies with whom they were in love.

Then she seemed to remember that somewhere
she had read a poem by Alexander Pope that had
spoken of those days.

It took her a little time to search back into her

memory for it because it was many years since she
had read the poem. Then she remembered.

> All, by the King's Example, liv'd and lov'd,
> Then Peers grew proud in Horsemanship t'excell,
> New-market's Glory rose, as Britain's fell.

She was quite pleased with herself when she
could repeat the three lines without, she was sure, a
mistake.

'I will tell Terry about it tomorrow,' she decided.

She found suddenly that she had been sitting so
long beside the little pond that she was in fact rather
cold.

She rose from the seat and started to walk back
towards the Inn.

As she did so she realised she was not alone
in the garden.

A number of gentlemen seemed to have over-
spilled onto the outside of one of the lighted windows
and she could see their white cravats and long-tailed
cut-away coats quite clearly.

They were talking loudly and laughing even
more loudly and as Orlena walked back towards the
Inn she felt apprehensive.

It was obvious that she would have to pass quite
close to them to find the door through which she had
come into the garden.

She hoped they would not notice her, but it was
a vain hope because the lights were full on her face
as she emerged from the shadows.

"By gad—a woman!" she heard one of the gentlemen ejaculate, and another added:

"And a pretty one, at that!"

Orlena quickened her pace, not looking at them
but vividly conscious that they were looking at her.

Then when only a few more steps would have
brought her to the door of the Inn they barred her
way.

"Who is this pretty lady I have not seen before?"
a gentleman asked.

His thick voice made Orlena realise he had been
drinking.

She looked up and her heart gave a frightened
leap as she saw that all the gentlemen—there must
have been six of them—were now between her and
the door.

They were, she saw, very young, and she was
certain they had been indulging freely. Several of
them held pewter mugs in their hands, and one man
carried a bottle.

They were, she knew, of her own class, and she
said coolly and quietly in a voice that she hoped
would not tremble:

"Let me pass, please, gentlemen."

"Where have you sprung from, pretty lady?"
asked the man who had spoken first. "And why have
we not met before?"

Orlena took a tentative step forward but realised
that the man standing directly in front of her had no
intention of moving.

"Not so quickly! Not so quickly!" he said. "We
want to talk to you. You must introduce yourself."

"I wish to enter the Inn . . . if you please," Orlena
replied.

She knew that her voice sounded a little breathless, but she held her chin high and hoped that the
men would have the decency to realise that she was
a lady.

"No, no, you do not want to go in there," a man
said. "It is overcrowded and noisy. You stay here with
us and we will look after you."

"Yes, that is what we will do," another one agreed.
"We will look after you and keep you safe from the
bears and bulls who will doubtless gobble you up!"

There was a burst of laughter at this, but Orlena
felt as if the gentlemen moved closer to her and instinctively she took a step backwards.

She was wondering whether she should turn and run away, but she had the uncomfortable feeling they would certainly run after her.

Then as she was wondering wildly what to do, a man opposite her said:

"I will tell you what, pretty lady. You shall go into the Inn if you will pay us for the privilege. A kiss is a fair price."

He put out his hand towards her as he spoke and Orlena gave a little cry of fright.

"No!" she said. "No, please . . . let me pass!"

Her voice was soft and breathless and she knew that now she was really frightened.

A young man's hand had almost touched her when a drawling voice behind them said:

"The lady said she wished to enter the Inn."

The men facing Orlena turned their heads.

As she followed the direction of their eyes she saw, standing outside the garden door which she herself wished to enter, the Corinthian.

If he had looked resplendent on the race-course, he looked even more magnificent now.

His white cravat and evening-shirt seemed quite dazzling in the darkness and she saw the glitter of his fob in the light from the window.

"What has it to do with—you?" asked the man carrying the bottle, who had previously taken no part in the conversation.

He was on the outside of the semi-circle that faced Orlena, but now he moved, saw who had spoken, and lapsed like the other gentlemen into an embarrassed silence.

Orlena was not quite certain how it happened, but as smoothly as the waters of the Red Sea parted to make a path for the Israelites, so the gentlemen moved out of her way.

Automatically she walked forward and she found herself standing beside the Corinthian. As she did so, she realised that her tormentors had vanished.

They had gone so swiftly that she had not even noticed them go.

Yet she saw now that the garden was empty except for herself and the man who had saved her.

"Thank . . . you," she said automatically, and the words were tremulous.

"Surely you should have enough sense not to come into the gardens of the Bushel on a night like this?" the Corinthian asked.

She looked at him wide-eyed, surprised at the stern note in his voice, despite the fact that he was drawling. The manner in which he seemed to tower above her was intimidating.

"There was . . . no-one here when I . . . walked down to the . . . pond," she said almost as if she must explain her actions to him.

"And what did you do when you reached it?" he enquired.

"I . . ."

She had begun to answer him, then realised it would be impossible to speak about the tune she had composed to this stranger of all men!

I . . . I think I . . . should go in," she said in a low voice.

"I think that would be a very unwise thing to do," he answered. "The Bushel is not the sort of place for a woman as young as you."

She looked up at him in surprise.

"B-but I am . . . staying here."

"Who with?"

The question was sharp.

"My . . . my brother."

She had a feeling, which she could not explain to herself, that he had expected her to say something else. After a moment he replied, still with that stern note in his voice:

"Your brother should have more sense, but I can see you come from the country."

There was no doubt that her gown told him that, Orlena thought, as his eyes flickered over it.

"Y-yes."

"From the North?"

"Y-yes."

She longed to tell him he had no right to inflict this catechism upon her; but somehow he mesmerised her, and although she wanted to leave him she was afraid to move away.

"I will escort you to the foot of the stairs," he said, "and another time, if you come to Newmarket, do not stay at the Bushel in race-week."

"I will ... not," Orlena replied, "and ... thank ... you."

She felt as if in some strange way he released her, and she walked towards the door.

She knew he was following her, and when she reached it they were for the moment out of the light from the windows and in the shadows.

Remembering that he had said he would see her to the stairs, and being suddenly afraid of the laughter and noise she heard coming from the Inn, she waited for him to open the door.

She glanced up at him and thought she had never seen a man who looked so cynical and so bored. Yet for the first time his firm mouth was twisted in a faint smile.

"You are very young and very lovely," he remarked. "I think I deserve your thanks and you should make them generous."

Her eyes widened in surprise, not knowing what he meant.

Then to her astonishment he put out his hand not to open the door, but to lift her chin with his fingers.

He raised her face towards his, and before she could move, before she could realise what was happening, his lips were on hers!

For a moment she was still with an utter astonishment which made it impossible for her to move. Then when she would have done so, she felt something strange, warm, and wonderful invade her whole body.

It was like a golden stream rushing from her lips down her throat and into her breasts.

It was so lovely, so perfect, that she felt as if the music she had heard in the garden, the fragrance of the flowers, and the velvet softness of the night passed from his lips into hers.

She could not explain, she could not move, it was almost impossible to breathe.

Then before she could collect her thoughts or realise what was happening he had set her free.

"Go back to the North, little Innocence," he said, "and make some bovine farmer happy."

As he spoke, he opened the door and they were inside.

The heat and noise struck her almost like a blow and she would have been unable to move if she had not felt the Corinthian's hand on her arm, propelling her towards the staircase.

They reached it, and as automatically Orlena's hand went out to clasp the oak stair-rail she heard him say in his clear, drawling voice:

"Go straight up and do not look back!"

As if under some strange spell which was impossible to break, she obeyed him.

She walked up the oak stairs and had the feeling that he was watching her go.

She reached her bed-room, slipped in through the door, and locked it behind her. Only then did her hands go up to her cheeks and she felt a blush diffuse her whole body.

* * *

Driving towards London, Orlena found it difficult to think of anything but what had happened last night.

When she undressed and got into bed she could hardly believe that what had happened to her downstairs had been real and not a figment of her imagination.

She had been kissed—kissed by a man whom she did not know—and she had made no effort to prevent him!

She had not struggled or protested, and she wondered if in fact she had been out of her mind.

How could she have allowed such a thing to happen? How for one moment could she have permitted herself to behave in such an outrageous fashion?

She tried to find an excuse by saying that she had been so frightened by the six men who had accosted her that she had been too weak to prevent the Corinthian from doing what he wished.

Yet she knew, if she was honest, that the wonder she felt had been the reason why she had not moved but had surrendered herself completely to the mastery of his lips.

It was he who had set her free.

"How could I do anything so reprehensible . . . so wicked?" Orlena asked herself.

She thought that Terry, if he knew the truth, would be ashamed of her, while her mother, if she were alive, would have been horrified.

"No-one must ever know," she told herself, but she knew that she would never forget what had occurred.

She had no idea that a kiss could be so perfect, so spiritually wonderful.

Always before she had shrunk from the idea of kissing a man, feeling that it was something far too intimate to contemplate with any of the men she had ever met or seen.

She had believed too that it would be an intrusion on the reserve which was an intimate part of her nature.

And yet brazenly she had stood still and let a man

hold her lips captive, while he had evoked in her a feeling so incredibly marvellous that even now she could feel the rapture of it pulsating through her.

'It was a part of the music I heard in the garden,' Orlena thought.

But knew that that was no excuse for her behaviour and that she should in fact feel thoroughly ashamed.

"You are very silent," Terry remarked as they drove towards Bishop's Stortford, where they were to change horses.

"What time did you get to bed?" Orlena asked quickly, to change the subject.

"I had a very interesting evening," Terry said. "We were, as it happens, Orlena, in exactly the right place."

"Were we?" she enquired, remembering what the Corinthian had said.

"Apparently the members of the Jockey Club and anyone else of importance in Newmarket for the races meet at the Bushel to celebrate their winnings or commiserate with each other over their losses."

'So that was why the Corinthian was there!' Orlena thought.

They had learnt on the race-course that he was a member of the Jockey Club. That too was why he had told her she should never come to the Bushel when racing was taking place on the Heath.

Terry was telling her of the information he had culled last night about the horses that were coming up for sale the following week in London.

"I shall go to Tattersall's as soon as I arrive," he said. "I do not want to miss some really good animals."

"The first thing we have to do is to find somewhere to live," Orlena reminded him.

"Yes, of course, but I dare say the Earl will be able to advise us."

Orlena looked at him in consternation.

"We must not impose on His Lordship's good

nature," she said. "Once he has agreed to our allowances, then we can be independent."

She paused before she added:

"And, Terry, I do not want to have anyone living with us. I am sure Mr. Thorogood's idea of a Chaperon is just a lot of old-fashioned nonsense."

"Yes, of course it is," Terry agreed reassuringly. "We will rent a house, Orlena, and I expect the Earl will put me up for White's and Brooks's if I ask him nicely."

He glanced at his sister to say almost crossly:

"I think you made a mistake in not buying yourself a decent gown in which to come to London. Compared with the women I saw yesterday on the Heath, you look like something out of Noah's Ark!"

"It was your idea to leave at once and do our spending when we reach London," Orlena replied defensively.

Terry had the decency to look somewhat shamefaced.

"I did think it best," he admitted. "At the same time, we have got to realise that the old man, if he takes a dislike to us, may be difficult over the money. It is only for three months as far as I am concerned, but I have no wish to waste time."

"No, of course not," Orlena agreed, "and I promise I will be very conciliatory. After all, I could always manage Papa . . . at least I thought I could."

"You were not very successful in getting money out of him," Terry said unkindly. "At the same time, I do not suppose that anyone could have done that."

"If he would not spend money on Mama he was not likely to spend any on me," Orlena said in a low voice.

She felt guilty.

Although Terry had not reproached her, she felt that in his heart he must think she had been singularly obtuse not to realise that they were not as poor as her father had made them out to be.

"How could I have known? How could I have guessed?" Orlena asked again as she had asked the question a thousand times already.

All the same, she knew she had been a failure in that respect, and she was determined, where the Earl of Ulverston was concerned, that she would do her very best for Terry.

They stopped at an Inn before they reached the outskirts of London and on Terry's instructions Orlena changed into what she considered was her best gown.

It did not look to her much better than the one she had been wearing, but it was of a softer, thinner material, which was why she had not travelled in it, and was the colour of forget-me-nots.

It had been one of her mother's summer gowns and Orlena had refurbished it as best she could in the short time she had before they left Weldon Park.

The touches of white at the wrists and the fichu at the neck with a broad satin sash to match round her waist made it very becoming even if it was very old-fashioned.

She tidied her hair and fluffed up the ribbons on her bonnet, but when she looked in the mirror she was sadly disappointed by her general appearance, although there was nothing she could do about it.

"Perhaps the Earl's sight will be failing," she told herself consolingly, "or perhaps he will like an unsophisticated young woman who will listen attentively to him."

She was well aware that that was what most elderly men wanted: someone to listen to their long stories and to fetch and carry, as her father had made her do towards the end of his life.

"Do not be apprehensive," she said to Terry when they set off once again on their journey, "I am sure everything will be all right. Papa used to speak very warmly of the Earl and thought of him as a good friend."

"I thought you said he had not mentioned him for years," Terry said suspiciously.

Orlena admitted to herself that she had exaggerated slightly, and she said quickly:

"Remember, we are not asking any favours of His Lordship. After all, we are both very rich. It is not as if we were impecunious hangers-on coming to beg him to support us."

"No, you are right," Terry said.

She thought that he squared his shoulders and his self-confidence returned.

At the same time, when they reached Ulverston House it was Orlena who felt nervous.

Situated in Park Lane, it was a very impressive mansion built of grey stone with a fine porticoed front door and high walls surrounding what was obviously a large garden.

Two stone griffons as it were guarded the entrance, and Orlena fancied that they looked scornfully at the shabby curricle as it passed between them.

However, Terry drew up his horses with a flourish and as a groom came running to their heads he and Orlena stepped out with commendable calm.

"We have called to see the Earl of Ulverston," Terry said to the footman who had opened the door.

A Butler came forward from the shadows of the Hall.

"You have an appointment, Sir?"

"Inform His Lordship that Sir Terence Weldon and Miss Orlena Weldon have arrived from Yorkshire to call on him!"

"I will inform His Lordship. Will you come this way, Miss?"

He spoke to Orlena and she followed the Butler across what she thought was the most magnificent Hall she had ever seen.

It had a marble floor, and fine curved staircases descending either side made it, she was sure, a perfect place in which to hold a party.

There were no less than six footmen in attendance and the Butler showed them into a Salon
which was decorated in blue and hung with pictures
which made Orlena look round her with delight.

Never had she seen such beautiful paintings, but
Terry remarked:

"His Lordship certainly lives in style! I am sure
of one thing: he never visited Weldon Park!"

"Look at the miniatures," Orlena said in an awed
voice, "and the china. I am sure it is *Sèvres*."

But Terry was not attending to her. He was, she
knew, thinking of the interview which lay ahead,
wondering how much the Earl would allow him to
spend immediately on the horses he wished to buy.

Quite a perceptible time elapsed before Orlena
asked nervously:

"Do you suppose the Earl is . . . here?"

"They would have told us if he was not," Terry
replied with common sense.

"Yes . . . of course."

She had not told her brother that it was a question which had presented itself to her insistently as
they grew nearer to London.

She had thought they had perhaps been too pre-
cipitate in leaving Yorkshire without first making certain that the Earl was in residence.

He might so easily be in the country, perhaps
staying with friends, and if it took them a long time
to get in touch with him, the hundred pounds which
Mr. Thorogood had given them might not cover their
expenses.

She had realised with some astonishment how expensive post-horses were, and the bills in the Inns
where they stayed seemed to be astronomical!

Terry had not told her whether or not he had lost
money at the races, but she could not help knowing
there must be very little left of the hundred pounds
they had started out with.

If they had to stay at an Hotel in London for any

length of time it would have to be a very cheap one.

Combined with these worries was the knowledge that they were far later in arriving than they had intended to be.

If the Earl was ailing, as her father had, he might retire to bed early.

Terry had intended to leave Newmarket at eight o'clock, but it had been nearly nine before the bill for their night's stay was presented and their curricle brought round from the stables.

Even so, the journey would not have taken so long if they had not been held up by an accident in Epping Forest.

A mail-coach had collided with a wagon carrying beer-barrels and the road was strewn with them, making it impossible for them to continue their journey until everything was cleared away.

As the drivers of the mail-coach and the wagon were engaged in a wordy argument over who had caused the accident, it was a long time before they could be prevailed upon to settle their differences.

It was impossible in the middle of the forest to make a detour or even to turn round, owing to the fact that quite a lot of traffic had closed up behind them, and finally it had been over two hours before they could proceed.

A further delay was due to the fact that the horses they had hired from the Posting-Inn at Bishop's Stortford were of a very inferior quality.

However cleverly Terry drove them, nothing would move them to exert themselves, and it was in fact six o'clock before they reached the outskirts of London.

If the Earl dined early, Orlena thought, he would in all probability very much resent being disturbed in the middle of his meal.

Then she told herself that London hours were quite different from those which prevailed in Yorkshire.

She had heard that the Prince of Wales ate at half past seven and she imagined that the rest of Society followed suit, but how could she be sure?

She was beginning to feel that something had gone wrong and the Earl was perhaps refusing to see them until the following morning, when the door of the Salon opened.

"His Lordship will see you now," the Butler said courteously.

They followed him, but this time they went down a broad corridor hung with portraits and decorated with some exceptionally fine furniture which even though she was worried Orlena could not help appreciating.

The Butler stopped in front of two large magnificently decorated double doors.

He flung them open and announced in stentorian tones:

"Sir Terence Weldon, M'Lord, and Miss Orlena Weldon!"

For a moment it was impossible for Orlena to be aware of anything but an enormous room which seemed to her to be decorated from floor to ceiling with books.

Then she was aware of three windows opening onto a flower-filled garden, and her eyes finally moved to a man standing with his back to the fireplace, watching their entry.

For a moment she could not credit the sight of her own eyes.

Then her heart started pounding fiercely and she felt a burning flush rising into her pale cheeks as she saw contemplating her with hard dark eyes under what seemed to be weary eye-lids the Corinthian who had kissed her in the garden last night!

Chapter Three

There was an uncomfortable silence, until Terry said:

"I think there is some mistake. I asked to see the Earl of Ulverston."

"I am the Earl of Ulverston!"

The Corinthian spoke in the drawling voice which Orlena remembered so well.

Then as Terry seemed astonished into silence he said:

"I think this needs some explanation. Perhaps you will both sit down."

He indicated a sofa at the side of the fireplace, and feeling as if her legs would not carry her Orlena walked towards it.

She could not look at him again.

She could not raise her eyes to meet the hard expression in his, and yet she was conscious that her heart was beating frantically and her breath was constricted in her throat.

She seated herself on the very edge of the sofa and clasped her fingers together in her lap.

She felt as if the whole world had turned a somersault, and that it was almost impossible for her to think coherently.

Terry walked to the fireplace but for the moment he did not sit down.

"The Earl of Ulverston was a friend of my father's," he said, "and approximately the same age."

"My father died two years ago."

"Then that would account for your being here," Terry said unnecessarily, "and I presume it also means that you are not our Guardian."

"That is something I have to explain to you," the Earl replied.

He looked at Terry, who almost as if obeying a command sat down in an arm-chair near to Orlena.

The Earl glanced at them both, but Orlena's eyes were downcast, her eye-lashes dark against her cheeks, which, now that the blush had gone, were paler than ever.

"When I returned from Newmarket today . . ." he began.

"How long did it take you?" Terry interrupted irrepressibly.

There was a faint twist to the Earl's lips as he answered.

"Four hours and fifty-two minutes!"

Terry gave a sigh.

"You had the horses. With the mules I had to drive I am only surprised we arrived at all."

The Earl did not reply and after a moment Terry said in a slightly embarrassed manner:

"I apologise, My Lord. I should not have interrupted you."

"As I was saying, when I returned from Newmarket I found a letter from your firm of Solicitors telling me of Sir Hamish Weldon's death, and informing me that his son and daughter were my Wards until they reached the age of twenty-one."

"Mr. Thorogood could not have known that your father was dead."

"That is obvious," the Earl replied loftily. "At the

same time it would have been wiser for him to have
made some enquiries before he sent you hot-foot to
London."

"It was our wish to come," Terry replied. "We
understand that until we meet our Guardian we are
not entitled to draw upon our inheritance."

"Your motive is understandable," the Earl remarked. "At the same time, until today I had no idea
of my father's commitment."

"Does this mean that we have in fact no Guardian?" Terry asked eagerly.

"That is what I myself anticipated to be the case,"
the Earl replied, "but unfortunately, owing to an act of
negligence on the part of your Solicitors, I am for the
moment your Guardian and you are in my charge."

"How can that be?" Terry asked truculently. "My
father thought he was leaving us in the hands of a
friend of his own age, someone he had known since
they had been at Oxford together."

"I have been informed of the circumstances, Sir
Terence," the Earl said, "and I have learnt that my
father accepted you as his responsibility when he was
asked to do so three years ago, after the death of your
mother."

"That is right," Terry agreed.

"But in making out the Deed of Guardianship
your Solicitors merely stated that you would be in
the care and under the jurisdiction of the Earl of
Ulverston."

Orlena was listening intently, but she still could
not look at the speaker.

"For some unknown reason, they omitted to
write 'the fourth Earl' after my father's name. Therefore," the Earl continued, "legally as the Earl of Ulverston at this present moment I automatically become responsible for you."

"That seems ridiculous!" Terry exclaimed.

"I agree with you whole-heartedly," the Earl replied, "but it happens to be a legal fact, and until we can get the Courts to agree to a dissolution of the Deed I am obliged to administer your fortune."

"Surely there should be no difficulty about a dissolution?" Terry asked.

"It will most regrettably entail our going to the Courts," the Earl answered, "and that will involve a certain amount of publicity. I have never thought it particularly desirable to have my private affairs discussed in public and I cannot believe that it is something that you would wish."

"No, of course not," Terry said quickly.

"In which case, until my Attorneys can find an easier way out of this tangle, I am afraid we shall have to accept things as they are."

"I can assure Your Lordship, my sister and I will be as little trouble as possible," Terry said, "but we need your permission to open a Bank Account and we require right away quite a considerable amount of spending money to be at our disposal."

"That I can understand," the Earl remarked.

Orlena felt that he was looking at their clothes and remembering the shabby curricle in which he had seen them on the race-course.

There was a sarcastic note in the Earl's voice which made her wince but Terry seemed unconscious of it.

"What I want most are horses," he said. "I want to set up my own stable and fill it with animals like the team you were driving. I have never seen finer horse-flesh!"

"You will be fortunate to find their like," the Earl replied, "but you will discover there are many people only too willing to provide you with acceptable horse-flesh, and naturally you will need to house them."

"My sister and I intend to rent a house in a fashionable part of London," Terry said boldly, "and we will of course choose one with adequate stabling attached to it."

The Earl did not speak and Terry went on:

"We have no desire, either of us, to be an en-cumbrance on Your Lordship. All we must have is your permission to go ahead, and if you will pro-vide us with the proper authority at the Bank we need trouble you no further."

"Your intentions are very clear to me," the Earl remarked, but it did not sound exactly a compliment. "You will doubtless also need to know the name of a good tailor."

Terry looked self-conscious, as if he was suddenly aware of the contrast he was to the man facing him.

The Earl had already changed into evening-clothes and Orlena thought he looked even more magnificent than he had the night before.

His intricately tied white cravat was a master-piece of ingenuity, and his long-tailed satin evening-coat fitted him so perfectly that he looked almost as if he had been poured into it.

Orlena was very conscious of what an authorita-tive, commanding figure he looked with his back against one of the most exquisite marble mantel-pieces she had ever seen.

There was a gilt-framed mirror above it and in it she could see the reflection of his square shoulders and his dark hair, which was arranged in the wind-swept fashion that had been set by the Prince of Wales.

She had read about it in the *Ladies' Journal* but now she was actually seeing it for herself.

"I should be very grateful for an introduction to your tailor, My Lord," Terry said in quite a humble tone, "and I hoped perhaps you might be kind enough to get me elected to the right Clubs."

"White's, I presume, and Brooks's," the Earl re-marked, "and like all the other young turnip-tops from the country you will try to throw away your for-tune on the green-baize tables."

Terry flushed at the repetition of the insult that

had been addressed to him by the Earl's groom as he moved their horses on the race-course.

"I assure Your Lordship I shall only gamble within my means," he said stiffly. "I am not so foolish as to dissipate my newly acquired wealth too quickly. I have lived in penury for too long."

The Earl raised his eye-brows and Terry said hotly:

"It is all very well for Your Lordship to sneer at us because we are raw from the country, but you may not have been informed that my father was a complete miser.

"My sister and I have never had two pennies to rub together until now. In fact I was expecting when my father died to have to sell my house and the Estate to keep us from starvation."

Terry's voice rose a little as he was speaking and Orlena bent towards him to say in a low tone:

"Terry . . . I beg of you . . ."

He looked at her, then as if he realised he was making an exhibition of himself he said quickly:

"I apologise, My Lord, but we have both suffered severely and unnecessarily these past years and you must excuse us if we are now anxious to forget the past."

"I was not aware of your circumstances," the Earl said, "but what you tell me only confirms my previous impression that you both need guidance. May I ask where you intend to stay tonight?"

Again Terry looked slightly embarrassed.

"I suppose it must be in an Hotel," he said, "and to tell Your Lordship the truth I have not much money left of the cash advanced to me by my Solicitors in Yorkshire."

"Then I hope you are looking to me to find you accommodation," the Earl said, "as I am not inclined to trust your judgement."

"May I ask why?" Terry enquired.

"Surely you are aware that you should not have

taken your sister to the Bushel in Newmarket when
there was racing on the Heath?" the Earl asked in a
tone of voice that made Orlena wince.

Terry looked surprised.

"It was the only Inn in which we could find rooms.
Was it wrong of us to stay there?"

"It certainly was!" the Earl replied briefly. "And
it is something I shall see will not happen again."

His eyes flickered over Orlena for a moment, and
she felt with a sudden constriction of her heart that
he was denouncing her behaviour in a manner only
she could understand.

Her fingers tightened on one another and she only
hoped that she did not appear as humiliated as she
felt, and that despite what he was thinking of her she
could continue to hold herself proudly.

"In the circumstances," the Earl went on, "considering how late it is in the evening, you must stay
here as my guests."

"We have no wish to be beholden to Your Lordship," Terry answered. "My sister and I will deal
quite well on our own. It is only a question of being
able to pay for wherever we may stay."

"As your Guardian," the Earl replied, "I must insist that your sister stays in respectable surroundings,
whatever you may feel in the matter."

"I am not being ungracious, My Lord," Terry
said quickly. "It is just that we have no wish to be
dependent upon your generosity."

"I know just what you were feeling, Sir Terence,"
the Earl said, "but this argument is quite unnecessary.
You will stay here and we will discuss your future
plans when I have more time to do so."

With an effort at good manners which made Orlena proud of him Terry replied:

"Then I can only thank Your Lordship and hope
that we shall incommode you as your guests tonight,
and as your Wards as little as possible."

"That of course is a different matter," the Earl

retorted. "But now I will introduce you both to some
guests I have staying in the house. I should add that
my mother, who is unfortunately unwell at the moment, lives with me and is therefore a very competent Chaperon for your sister."

There was a moment's pause. Then Terry said a
little hesitantly:

"We were—hoping, My Lord, that if we took a
house of our own, it would be unnecessary for my
sister to have—a Chaperon."

"Do you really imagine that if your sister desires
to meet the *Beau Monde* she will be accepted as a
young woman living on her own?"

"I see no harm in it," Terry said defensively.

"You may not," the Earl replied, and there was no
doubt that once again he was sneering. "But if you
wish your sister to be the prey of every fortune-hunter,
roué, and charlatan of the town, I can imagine no
better way to do it than to set her up in an establish-
ment without a proper Chaperon and someone to instruct her in the manners of the Social World."

Orlena felt the colour rising in her cheeks.

She was very sensible of the fact that as far as
she was concerned almost every word the Earl spoke
had a sharp edge to it.

It was obvious what he thought of her behaviour
last night and she wished that the floor would open
beneath her and swallow her up.

As the clock on the mantelpiece chimed, the Earl
turned his head to look at it and said sharply:

"I have no time for further discussion. I will order
the servants to bring in your luggage, and if you will
both come with me I will present you to the Duchess
of Dorset, who is staying here as my guest."

He did not wait for a reply but moved across
the room towards the door. Orlena, rising, made to follow him and as she did so she exchanged a glance
with Terry.

She realised he was resenting the high-handed

manner in which the Earl had settled their movements.

She told herself, however, that they had no alternative but to obey his orders, even though he issued them in a somewhat unpleasant manner.

'He is our Guardian,' she thought. 'There is nothing we can do without him.'

Yet how could anybody have imagined outside a melodrama that the Corinthian who had treated them so scornfully on the race-course and the man who had kissed her last night would turn out to be the Earl of Ulverston?

'I cannot stay here for long,' she thought frantically as the Earl escorted them down the broad passage towards the Hall.

When they reached it he stopped outside a pair of double doors manned by two footmen, who opened them, and Orlena walked beside him into a most magnificent and luxurious Salon.

It was furnished in the French style and, uncomfortable though she was feeling and nervous at the Earl's proximity, she knew as she walked over the beautiful Savonnerie carpet that it was just the sort of room she had dreamt of and thought never to see.

At the far end in front of the fireplace there were two women, the older one wearing a profusion of diamonds.

This, Orlena knew, must be the Duchess of Dorset, and she felt dazzled by the magnificent tiara on her white hair and the necklace of glittering jewels round her neck.

"We have, Duchess, two unexpected guests tonight," the Earl said as they reached the hearth-rug. "May I present my Ward, Miss Orlena Weldon, and her brother, Sir Terence."

As Orlena sank down in a low curtsey the other woman standing beside the Duchess gave a little cry of astonishment.

"Your Ward? I had no idea you had one."

"Nor had I until today," the Earl drawled.

"Where can they have come from?"

"Now there was not so much astonishment in the young voice as an almost irrepressible laughter, and looking up Orlena saw that the speaker was in fact a girl of perhaps her own age, although the difference in their appearance was overwhelming.

"Let me introduce you," the Earl said. "Lady Adelaide Darlington—Miss Orlena Weldon!"

Orlena put out her hand but Lady Adelaide did not appear to see it.

She was looking at Orlena's gown and bonnet and now she obviously found it impossible to restrain her mirth.

"You certainly do not look the type of Wards I would have expected His Lordship to own," she said. "Where can you have come from?—no, do not tell me—it is not hard to guess . . ."

"And Sir Terence Weldon—" the Earl interposed.

The laughter on Lady Adelaide's lips and in her eyes was mitigated a little when she looked at Terry. Now she held out her hand and as he bowed over it she said:

"I feel this must be your first visit to London."

She was, Orlena had to admit, extremely beautiful, with dark hair arranged in the latest fashion and a high-waisted gauze gown which revealed every curve of her perfect figure.

She seemed like a being from another world and Orlena was humiliatingly conscious of her own appearance.

"My Wards are staying here with me," the Earl said, "and I think in the circumstances we must send a message to the Marchioness of Crewe to say that we unfortunately cannot dine with her tonight."

"No, please do not do that," Orlena interposed quickly. "We have been travelling all day and I would, if Your Lordship would permit it, prefer to go to bed immediately."

"If that is what you wish," the Earl replied, "it is of course quite easily arranged."

"I would much prefer it, and you must certainly not alter your plans," Orlena said.

"You can hardly suggest, Blair, that we take your new responsibilities with us," Lady Adelaide said to the Earl in an audible aside.

There was no mistaking the fact that she intended to be unpleasant.

As if she felt her daughter was being tactless the Duchess said gently:

"I am sure Miss Weldon is right. After a long journey all one wants is rest. But if we do not intend to keep the dinner-party waiting I think we should leave at once."

"Very well," the Earl conceded. "I will ask Mr. Greville, the Comptroller of my household, to look after you, Sir Terence, and tomorrow he will see to your other requirements."

There was no doubt what those were, and Terry bowed a brief acknowledgement. The Duchess looked at Orlena and said kindly:

"I shall see you tomorrow, Miss Weldon. I hope you pass a peaceful night."

Orlena curtseyed, but as Lady Adelaide followed her mother she heard a barely repressed giggle and felt a sudden resentment against this young woman who had made her feel even more humiliated than she did already.

Yet there was no doubt that Lady Adelaide was beautiful.

Tall, she walked with a regal dignity and grace and gave the Earl as she passed him a provocative and intimate glance as if she was inviting him to laugh with her at these country bumpkins.

But the Earl paused before he followed her.

"If you will remain here," he said to Orlena, "my Housekeeper will show you to your room. Please ask her for anything you need."

"Thank ... you," Orlena managed to murmur.

Despite an inner resolution, she found herself looking up into the Earl's face and found that his hard dark eyes were looking penetratingly down at her.

She had the feeling, although she was not sure, that he was searching for something. It was only a quick impression, because shyness made her drop her eyes again.

Then he was walking away down the room.

The door of the Salon closed behind them and Terry made an exclamation half of irritation and half of relief.

"God!" he ejaculated. "I feel as if I have been squashed flat by an overloaded wagon! How the devil can we have got ourselves in a position like this?"

"How could we imagine for one moment that Papa's friend would die and the man we had seen at Newmarket would turn out to be our Guardian?" Orlena replied.

"And what a Guardian!" Terry groaned. "He is not going to make things easy, I can see that, Orlena!"

She gave a little shiver.

"I do not want to stay here, Terry, not with the Duchess and that horrible girl. She was laughing and sneering at us ..."

Orlena stopped.

"It was not without reason, I admit," she added honestly. "We must both look figures of fun."

"That is not our fault," Terry said savagely, "and nothing is going to stop me from buying some decent clothes tomorrow, I can promise you that!"

"I ... think it is ... worse for me," Orlena said in a very small voice, but he did not seem to hear her.

Orlena went to bed feeling, despite the attentions of two experienced maids and the elegance of her bed-room, in the very depths of depression.

It had been bad enough living with her father and going without every form of necessity, let alone luxury; but now it was even worse to feel she was in an alien world and that everything she did was wrong.

And yet as she felt like crying in the darkness it was impossible not to remember the wonder of the Earl's kiss even though to him it had been an entirely insignificant action.

That he condemned her behaviour was quite obvious, and while Orlena condemned it herself she knew that nothing could take away from her what she had felt.

It had been a rapture that had seemed to incorporate in one sensation everything beautiful she had ever thought, seen, or heard in music.

"Terry is right, we cannot stay here," she told herself, "and even if the Earl insists on my having a Chaperon, at least it will mean I will not have to see him."

She thought that actually she hated him for his mockery, his cynicism, and his disapproval. Yet at the same time he was responsible for the magic that she knew she could never forget.

She was, however, so tired after the journey and having lain awake a long time the night before in the Bushel that she was surprised when the maid drew back the curtains to find that it was nearly nine o'clock.

This, Orlena told herself, was certainly keeping town hours!

Breakfast was brought to her on a tray.

While she drank the delicious coffee and ate what was prepared for her on the silver dish on which was embellished the Earl's crest, she thought how much she would enjoy her surroundings if they belonged to anyone else except him.

The Housekeeper, whom she had met the night before, a kindly woman with grey hair and dressed in rustling black, knocked on the door as soon as Orlena had finished breakfast.

She curtseyed respectfully and advancing towards the bed said:

"Her Grace's compliments, Miss, and she asked me to inform you that on His Lordship's instructions she is waiting to take you shopping in an hour's time."

Orlena was silent for a moment. She had no wish to go shopping with the Duchess. At the same time, she was aware that it was unlikely that the Earl would permit her to go alone, and even if he did she had no idea where she should go.

With an effort she managed to reply:

"Will you ... please thank ... Her Grace ... and say I will not ... keep her waiting."

"Before you leave, Miss," the Housekeeper went on, "Her Ladyship would be pleased to make your acquaintance."

For one moment Orlena thought she was referring to Lady Adelaide; then the Housekeeper explained:

"His Lordship's mother, Miss, the Dowager Countess. She's confined to her own apartments, but I'll take you there as soon as you're dressed."

"Thank you," Orlena answered.

She wished after she had bathed that she had something fashionable to put on. And she regretted again that Terry had not allowed her to buy at least one new gown in York before they came South.

It might have delayed them only for two days, and she would not have felt so ashamed of her appearance as the Housekeeper took her through the long, elaborately furnished passages.

At the same time, because Orlena was sensitive to environment, she knew that everything she saw had an exceptional quality about it.

She could not help her senses responding to the pictures, to the vases of flowers which stood everywhere, and to the air of elegance and luxury, which was quite different from anything she had seen before.

The Dowager Countess's room seemed to be filled

with flowers, and the huge bed, draped in silk, was overpowering.

But its occupant had, Orlena thought, one of the sweetest faces she had ever seen, and the smile with which the Countess greeted her was somehow reminiscent of Orlena's mother.

"My son Blair has told me all about you, Miss Weldon," she said. "How exciting it must be for you and your brother to come to London for the first time. I do hope we will be able to help you enjoy yourselves."

It was impossible for Orlena not to respond to such kindness.

"Thank you, Ma'am," she answered, "but it is all very strange and I am well aware how countrified and gauche I and my brother look."

"That is the last word I would have applied to you," the Countess said gently. "Sit down, child, and tell me about yourself. I gather from my son that your father and mother are both dead."

"Mama died three years ago," Orlena answered, "and I think now that Papa must have become a little strange when she left us. He had always been somewhat cheese-paring over money, but then he grew quite fanatical on the subject."

It was so easy to talk to this sympathetic elderly woman that before Orlena realised what was happening she had told her everything. How worried they had been when her father died that they would have to sell the house and the Estate; how little they had had to eat; how Terry had resented not being able to do any of the things his friends could do.

"He had no horses to ride, Ma'am," she said, "and you know how much that means to a man."

"I do indeed," the Countess said. "But now everything has changed and you can both look forward to a very different future."

"That is what I want to do," Orlena said, "but I

am afraid Terry and I may make a great many mistakes."

"My son will see that your brother makes as few
as possible," the Countess replied, "and I have already
spoken to my dear friend the Duchess of Dorset about
your clothes. Blair told me that you need a whole
trousseau."

Orlena felt herself flush.

She was well aware how sarcastic the Earl would
have been about her appearance.

"I can imagine nothing more exciting than being
able to buy everything you need," the Countess went
on, "knowing that you need not trouble yourself about
the expense. How lovely to have everything new without feeling guilty of extravagance!"

Orlena smiled.

"You are making it sound such fun, Ma'am, but I
had in fact been rather apprehensive that I would
not know how to start."

"You can trust the Duchess," the Countess told
her. "We were girls together, and I can tell you that
Her Grace as a girl was very beautiful, very frivolous,
and very, very dress-conscious."

It made the rather awe-inspiring Duchess seem
quite human, and when finally Orlena went down the
stairs to join her she was by no means as nervous as
she had been before.

To her complete relief there was no sign of Lady
Adelaide, nor as it happened of anyone else.

Orlena had already learnt from the Housekeeper
that Terry had gone out very early, and she guessed it
would be first to visit a tailor and then to Tattersall's.

She found the Duchess waiting in the Salon and
they drove away from Ulverston House in an extremely smart town cabriolet drawn by two superb horses.

The Duchess was looking very smart, and her
jewels, which matched the colour of her gown, were
very impressive.

Because of what the Countess had told Orlena

she seemed less awe-inspiring than she had the night before, and she showed great understanding as she started to make a list of everything Orlena would require.

"We will go first to Bond Street," she said. "There are dozens of things we shall wish to order; but we must also try to find you something to wear immediately, and for that we may be forced to visit some of the bigger stores that cater for those who are impatient or come to London for only a quick visit."

There was however a profusion of choice at the dressmakers, who were all within easy distance of one another in Bond Street.

There was such a wide variety of exquisite materials that Orlena thought she would never have made up her mind if she had not had the Duchess to advise her.

Even so, she grew bewildered at the amount of things that Her Grace considered essential, and after a time she lost count of everything that was ordered and only hoped when the bills were presented she would have enough money to meet them.

Then she told herself that she was rich—an heiress! In fact she had so much money it seemed impossible that she would ever be able to spend it all.

As if the Duchess knew what she was thinking she said kindly:

"We may seem to be buying a lot, but remember, we are starting from scratch. I wish I could do that myself."

Orlena looked at her in surprise.

"I have a large family, Miss Weldon, and although my husband is a wealthy man he has very many demands made upon his purse. Of course my sons, like your brother, want horses, which run away with all their allowance, and my married daughters have children, who all expect Grandmama to provide for them. So when I do buy myself something entirely frivolous, I feel quite guilty!"

Orlena laughed and from that moment she felt almost as friendly towards the Duchess as she did towards the Earl's mother.

When finally some hours later they left Bond Street Orlena was dressed in the very latest fashion.

She felt a little embarrassed at how revealing the straight gown was, and she had in fact been quite shocked at how much her figure showed in those that were to be worn in the evening.

She voiced her fears, but both the dressmaker and the Duchess had waved them aside.

"You have a very good figure, Miss," the dressmaker had said. "The only impropriety I can see in the new fashion is that it reveals those who are fat in the wrong places."

"There are quite a number of those," the Duchess remarked.

"That is true, Your Grace. It often seems to me that the worse her figure, the more a woman seems to want to draw attention to it."

"I am sure this gown should have an extra lining," Orlena said unhappily.

"I will put one in, Miss," the dressmaker replied, "but I am quite certain that once you have got used to being *de rigeur* you will ask me to take it out again."

Orlena felt this was unlikely and she insisted, despite everything the dressmaker said, in raising the neckline of her gowns and having them lined with a thicker material than was usual.

Nevertheless, she could not help feeling pleased with herself when finally, in a gown of very pale spring-green gauze which seemed to give her green lights in her eyes, and a bonnet with a high crown trimmed with small, tightly curled ostrich-feathers of the same colour, they drove back to Ulverston House.

"I do hope Terry is there when I get back," Orlena told the Duchess excitedly. "I doubt if he will recognise me."

However, it was not Terry who was standing in the Hall when they entered the house, but the Earl.

Immediately on seeing him Orlena felt self-conscious and was even more afraid than she had been before that her gown revealed too much of her figure.

"We have had a most enjoyable morning, Blair," the Duchess said. "If there is one thing which really delights me it is being able to spend somebody else's money."

"I am sure you have been very helpful to Miss Weldon," the Earl replied.

Orlena looked at him, her eyes very wide under her new bonnet.

He spoke in his drawling, rather bored fashion, and she could not tell whether he approved or disapproved. She only knew she was actually conscious of him and because his eyes were on her she felt shy.

"I think," she said in a soft, hesitating little voice, "that ... I will ... go upstairs and show myself to the ... Countess."

She spoke to the Duchess, but the Earl replied:

"I am sure my mother would like you to do that. She has already informed me that she approves wholeheartedly of my new responsibility."

Orlena glanced at him to see if he was being sarcastic, then decided he was speaking sincerely and felt a sudden flicker of warmth towards him.

She turned towards the stairs, then hesitated and moved back towards the Duchess.

"I want to thank you again, Ma'am," she said. "You have been kind ... so very kind."

"It has been a great pleasure, dear child," the Duchess replied, and without looking again at the Earl, Orlena ran up the stairs.

It was later in the afternoon that the joy she felt in her new clothes and her new appearance was dispersed by Lady Adelaide.

She had not appeared at luncheon, nor had Terry, and Orlena lunching alone with the Earl and the Duchess had found herself talking quite naturally of her life in Yorkshire and how they had been forced to eat rabbit until they were heartily sick of the animal, and yet had been able to afford nothing else.

"It reminds me what I suffered when I was in the Army . . ." the Earl began.

Even the Duchess had some story of privation and hunger, which made Orlena find that she enjoyed the meal more than she had thought possible.

It was difficult not to feel afraid of the Earl and occasionally there was that mocking note in his voice which made her feel very small, or the sarcastic note which made her wince.

But he was in fact in quite a genial mood and when he left them after the meal was over the Duchess said:

"I have never known Blair so good-humoured. I think after all he may be considering his mother's wish that he should settle down and get married."

"Get married?" Orlena exclaimed.

"It is really a secret," the Duchess explained, "but there has been an understanding between our families that he should marry Adelaide. This is her second Season in London and now that she has found her feet, so to speak, my dear friend the Countess thought it expedient that we should come and stay and that the two young people should get to know each other."

Orlena did not speak and after a moment the Duchess went on:

"Of course Blair is eight years older than Adelaide, but then they have known each other ever since they were children, and in my opinion, the most important thing in any marriage is to have the same background and the same interests."

She smiled reminiscently as she added:

"It is what my husband and I had, and of course

Adelaide will look very beautiful in the Ulverston diamonds."

"I am sure she will," Orlena said.

She did not know why but she felt as if the sun was slightly overcast and the room not as bright as it had been.

The Duchess told her she was going to call on some friends and left Orlena alone.

She went immediately to find the Earl's Secretary, Mr. Greville, having guessed that he was the person who could help her to find what she required.

She had already learnt from something the Earl had said that the Secretary's room was near the Library.

The footman opened the door for her and she entered to find Mr. Greville seated at a desk surrounded by deed-boxes and filing cabinets, while the walls were covered with maps of the Earl's various Estates.

He rose as Orlena entered and she said nervously:

"I ... I am not disturbing you? His Lordship said I might ask you for ... anything I ... required."

"I shall be only too happy to be of any assistance," Mr. Greville replied.

He was a man of about thirty-six and had, Orlena thought, an air about him which made her quite certain that he had at one time been a soldier.

She was to learn later that she was correct in this assumption.

She crossed the room to sit down in front of the desk.

"I expect Terry has already been here asking you innumerable questions," she began.

"Your brother is fully occupied having himself fitted out to rival even Beau Brummel, and is determined to purchase horses which he hopes will make His Lordship's look like Army mules!"

Orlena laughed.

"Terry was always ambitious."

"He is indeed," Mr. Greville agreed. "And what are your ambitions, Miss Weldon?"

"I want books. I want to buy or borrow a lot of books," Orlena answered, "and to ask if it would be possible and no trouble to anybody if I could play the pianoforte."

"But of course," Mr. Greville agreed. "There are several in the house. The one in the Music-Room is an exceptional instrument, and there is one in the Blue Drawing-Room, where I think you will find it more pleasant to practise if that is what you intend to do."

"I thought . . . after we settled somewhere," Orlena said a little tentatively, "that I could have . . . lessons . . . if you could advise me where I could procure a good teacher."

"I cannot think of one offhand," Mr. Greville replied, "but I will make enquiries and I am certain we can find somebody to your satisfaction."

"Thank you very much," Orlena said, "and what about the books?"

"The Library is filled with every sort of volume. In fact His Lordship buys practically every book of significance that is published."

"May I borrow them?" Orlena asked.

"I am sure he will be delighted. Shall I take you there now and show you where the latest volumes have been placed?"

"If it would be no trouble," Orlena replied.

Mr. Greville took her to the Library and she found there were shelves of books that had all been published in the last five years and which she immediately wanted the chance of reading.

There were all the newspapers too and as her eyes lit up at the sight of them Mr. Greville said:

"I must apologise that you did not receive the newspapers this morning when you were called. His Lordship always insists that every guest should be called with the papers and you will find tomorrow morning both the *Times* and the *Morning Post* on your breakfast-tray."

"That is the most luxurious thing I have ever heard!" Orlena exclaimed. "When we had the newspapers at home Papa would never allow Mama or me to read them until he had read them himself."

"People are often extraordinarily mean in small things," Mr. Greville answered. "His Lordship is very generous in that way, and as it happens in a great many others!"

Orlena thought it would be impertinent to question him further, but with Mr. Greville's permission she took a book and a newspaper from the Library and carried them with her to the Salon.

She had just seated herself down to read them when the door opened and Lady Adelaide came in.

She was looking even more beautiful than she had the night before.

Her dark flashing eyes would have made any face attractive, just as her regal carriage and the shape of her head would have been noticeable even in a room thronged with beautiful women.

She walked towards Orlena, who because she felt nervous rose to her feet.

"I have come to have a look at you," Lady Adelaide said. "I hear Mama has transformed the country bumpkin with a touch of her magic wand!"

Lady Adelaide spoke in a somewhat unpleasant manner, but Orlena told herself it would be stupid to take offence.

"Your mother has been very kind," she said. "I am extremely grateful to Her Grace."

"So you should be!" Lady Adelaide said. "How soon will you and your brother be leaving Ulverston House?"

"I am afraid I do not know."

"Shall I say that as far as I am concerned the sooner the better?" Lady Adelaide enquired. "Quite frankly, Miss Weldon, I do not like women, and although it is not a question of competition I would prefer to see the back of you as quickly as possible!"

The high-handed way in which she spoke made Orlena feel angry. At the same time, she told herself she had no right to be anything but polite.

"My brother is anxious that we should rent a house together," she said. "It is only a question of waiting for our Guardian's permission."

"I will speak to him myself," Lady Adelaide said complacently. "That gown must have cost you a pretty penny. I suppose your much-vaunted fortune really does exist? You certainly did not look like an heiress last night."

"We had come straight from the country, as you realise," Orlena replied, "and the Earl will be able to inform you more accurately concerning my fortune than I am able to do myself."

She thought this was almost a shrewd thrust, but Lady Adelaide said in sulky tones:

"I have no wish to discuss you with the Earl. The sooner he forgets your existence, the better. I expect my mother has told you that we are to marry each other?"

"Then I must congratulate you," Orlena said.

"It is of course a secret," Lady Adelaide said sharply, "and kindly do not speak of it to the Earl. We neither of us wish to be talked about at present."

"I understand," Orlena said.

She picked up her book and her newspaper.

"If you will excuse me," she said, "I wish to read. I think I will go to my own room."

"Your *own* room?" Lady Adelaide said sharply. "That is just the sort of attitude of which I am afraid. You and your brother are settling yourselves in here and I do not like it. You will make arrangements to leave as soon as possible."

Orlena stared at her in bewilderment and with an effort forced herself to speak calmly and gently.

"As I have already explained, Lady Adelaide, it entirely depends on our Guardian. But I would like to make this clear—neither my brother nor I wish to stay where we are not wanted!"

She did not wait to hear Lady Adelaide's reply but walked as quickly as possible from the Salon, closing the door sharply behind her.

"How could anybody be so unpleasant?" she asked as she went upstairs.

Then insidiously the thought came to her that if that was the sort of woman the Earl admired no wonder he thought her insignificant!

Chapter Four

Orlena was playing the pianoforte, gradually losing herself in the music so that she was oblivious of everything else.

She had now been staying at Ulverston House for nearly two weeks and she had got into the way of calling on the Dowager Countess in the morning and in the evening, and she also dropped in to see her at other times when she had nothing special to do.

She realised that the older woman was lonely, and there was no pretence about the welcome she received as soon as she appeared in the doorway of the bed-room.

"Come in, my dear," the Countess would say. "Tell me what you have been doing. You know I am longing to hear every detail of the Ball last night."

It was like being with her mother, Orlena thought, and she told the Countess of the compliments that had been paid to her and what she had thought of the various parties at which the Duchess had chaperoned her.

She realised it was on the Earl's instructions that the Duchess had arranged for her to be invited to all the important Balls and large Receptions which were taking place because it was the Season.

At first Orlena had felt very shy, especially as she thought that Lady Adelaide would resent her being included in the parties and suspect her of having contrived to bring it about.

But Lady Adelaide had her own friends and as it happened they were seldom in the same dinner-party.

In fact, Orlena usually had only fleeting glances of her surrounded by admirers at the Balls or being singled out at Receptions by the most distinguished guests.

She thought sometimes that the Duchess really enjoyed having someone like herself to chaperon, whom she could instruct and supervise and introduce as if she were her special protégée.

Orlena was sensible enough to be aware that the interest most people had in her came largely from the fact that she was known to be an heiress.

She also received a large number of compliments and much attention from gentlemen who squired her into dinner and with whom she danced.

But she found that the more fulsome and flattering they were, the more the Duchess dismissed them as possible suitors by telling her that they were undoubtedly fortune-hunters.

What surprised her was that she in fact saw very little of the Earl.

She learnt that he disliked Balls, was in constant attendance upon the Prince of Wales, and was more concerned with racing and riding his horses than being a part of the Social Scene.

"Everybody tries to inveigle His Lordship to their parties," the Duchess told Orlena, "but the hostesses think themselves lucky if he so much as puts in an appearance, and he always makes an excuse to leave early."

Orlena, who had felt that he might be looking out for her to behave in a reprehensible manner or disapprove of something she did, found in fact that she was relieved by his absence.

However, she was not certain if it was genuinely as much of a relief as she had thought it would be.

Whenever she met him in the house he looked magnificent and at the same time as cynical and bored as he had the first time she saw him on the race-course.

While she kept meaning to ask him how soon she and Terry could leave Ulverston House, the opportunity of a private conversation never seemed to present itself.

There was no doubt that Terry was completely happy.

The Earl, Orlena learnt, had offered him the hospitality of his stables and he was entirely concerned with buying horses and enjoying the Clubs to which the Earl had introduced him.

"I do not think we ought to stay here too long," Orlena had said to him last night.

"What is the hurry?" Terry enquired. "We are extremely comfortable—at least I am—and I have no time at the moment, Orlena, to go house-hunting, even if His Lordship would permit it."

"Do you mean he might refuse to let us set up house on our own?"

"I think he might easily do that," Terry replied. "Besides, how could you want a better or more distinguished Chaperon than the Duchess?"

This was an irrefutable argument, but remembering Lady Adelaide's attitude Orlena could not help thinking uncomfortably that she was monopolising too much of her mother's time.

"I shall have to make Terry speak to the Earl," she told herself, knowing that she was finding it impossible to speak to him herself and would in fact be rather afraid to do so.

When they were not dining with various distinguished and important hostesses, there were big dinner-parties at Ulverston House.

Orlena thought that the guests on these occasions
were far more interesting than those she met elsewhere, and she decided it was because in most cases
the gentlemen she sat next to at dinner were older
and more intelligent.

They, however, like the Earl, seldom danced,
and at Balls she was invariably partnered by very
young men whose conversation she found extremely
boring.

Today she had excused herself from accompany-
ing the Duchess to a huge Reception given by the
Marchioness of Torrington, and after spending a little
time reading one of the latest books from His Lordship's Library she had gone to the Countess's room
to receive her usual welcome.

"I am afraid I will not be very good company
today, my dear," the Countess said in her gentle
voice. "I had a bad night, and therefore have a tiresome head-ache."

"Would you like me to play to you, Ma'am?"
Orlena asked. "Mama often found it soothing when
her head ached."

"I would love it!" the Countess replied.

Orlena already knew that there was a pianoforte
in the *Boudoir* which was next to the Countess's bed-
room.

She opened the doors between the two rooms
and sat down at the piano, thinking as she did so how
attractive the Sitting-Room looked and how fragrant
the flowers which decorated it smelt.

But as soon as she touched the keys she found
herself unable to think of anything but the music she
could create and through which she found it easy to
express her secret thoughts and feelings.

She played first several classical pieces. Then as
if she could not resist it she played some of the melodies she had composed herself.

Each one conjured up a picture of when it had

come to her. Sometimes after her father had been more difficult and fault-finding than usual, the melodies had calmed and soothed her.

There was one which brought back her mother so vividly because after she had heard it she had encouraged Orlena to go on composing.

Then, irresistibly it seemed to her, she found herself playing the melody which had come to her mind the night she had stayed at the Bushel and had gone into the garden to sit beside the little waterlily pond.

The music had come to her, she felt, from the fragrance of the flowers and the velvet darkness of the night.

But now it was indivisible from the emotions that the Earl's lips had aroused in her when he had held hers captive.

The music brought back the incredible sensation of rapture and wonder she had felt and as Orlena finished playing she felt almost as if she still quivered from the touch of him.

She gave a little sigh and dropped her hands onto her lap. As she did so a voice said:

"I had no idea you were so talented!"

She started and found she was not alone as she had thought, for seated in an arm-chair, lying back very much at his ease with his legs crossed, was the Earl!

His presence had seemed so vivid when she was playing that for a moment she could only stare at him wide-eyed, not quite certain if he was real or still part of the fantasy the music had conjured up.

"My mother is asleep," he said, "for which I imagine I must thank you."

Orlena glanced towards the door into the Countess's room and realised the Earl had shut it.

"I want to talk to you, Orlena."

Although she had been about to rise, Orlena re-

mained seated on the music-stool and looked at him
a little apprehensively.

"I understand that you refused to accompany the
Duchess this afternoon," the Earl said, "and on several occasions, including the night before last, you did
not accept the invitations which were extended
to you. Why?"

The last word seemed to be spoken sharply and
although Orlena was not looking at the Earl she was
aware that he was watching her with his penetrating
dark eyes, which always made her feel shy.

"This afternoon I ... thought it would be ... nice
to be with ... your mother," she said after a moment.

"My mother has told me frequently how much
she appreciates your visits," the Earl replied, "but
surely that excuse does not apply to the party you
might have attended on Tuesday."

Orlena hesitated and was conscious that the colour was rising in her cheeks.

"I had ... a book which I was ... very interested
in ... reading," she said. "It was ... one which came
from ... Your Lordship's Library."

"Are you telling me that you prefer to sit at home
and read a book, or to play to my mother, rather than
be a guest in one of the most fashionable houses in
London?"

The surprise in the Earl's voice was unmistakable.

Orlena rose from the music-stool and walked towards a chair that was opposite the one occupied by
the Earl.

"It may seem very ... strange to you," she said
after a moment in a hesitating little voice, "but I am
... not used to so much ... gaiety ... and because I
have been ... alone so much in my ... life, I would
sometimes ... much rather stay at ... home."

She paused for a moment to add hastily:

"Please ... do not think it rude of me after you

have been so kind . . . in asking the Duchess to chaperon me . . . I am grateful . . . I am really! It is just that it is . . . too much . . . all at once."

She looked at the Earl pleadingly as if she begged him to understand, and after a moment's pause he said:

"You surprise me, Orlena!"

He did not sound angry, and, feeling that this was the opportunity for which she had been waiting, Orlena said:

"I wanted to ask Your Lordship when you would . . . wish Terry and me to leave?"

"You are not comfortable at Ulverston House?"

"Yes . . . yes, of course, I never imagined any place could be so luxurious or everyone so . . . kind," Orlena replied. "It is just that we do not wish to be an . . . encumbrance upon you."

"Have I given you the impression that you might be?"

He was making it difficult, Orlena thought, and she said hastily:

"You have been more generous than I could possibly have expected. Terry has told me how you are stabling his horses, that you have introduced him to the Clubs that he longed to join; and you arranged for Her Grace to look after me."

"But you still wish to be on your own?" the Earl said. "Do you really consider you are competent to cope with the Social World without guidance?"

"I was not . . . thinking of the . . . Social World," Orlena answered.

"Then what world?" he enquired.

Orlena clasped her hands together.

She felt it was almost impossible to explain what she did feel, and she was at the moment only acutely conscious that the Earl was watching her and she was not certain whether or not he was irritated by what she had asked.

After a moment he said:

"I think it would be in the best interests of both you and your brother to leave things as they are at the moment. The Duchess enjoys looking after you, so you need have no fears on that score, and my mother also likes having you here. I think she would miss you now if you left."

"Then ... I shall be very pleased to stay," Orlena replied. "It is ... just that I would not wish to ... impose upon Your Lordship's generosity ... or to upset ... Lady Adelaide."

"What has Lady Adelaide to do with it?" the Earl enquired sharply.

Orlena remembered that she had been told not to mention the fact that he and Lady Adelaide were to be married.

Too late she wished she had not mentioned her.

"When the Season is over," the Earl went on, "we can discuss what you and your brother wish to do. I understand from what he has said that there are a great many repairs and alterations to be done at Weldon Park."

"Yes ... of course."

"Then shall we leave everything as it is until His Royal Highness goes to Brighton at the beginning of June?" the Earl asked. "After that, London will gradually empty and we can decide what is best where you are concerned."

"I should be very ... glad to do ... that," Orlena said, feeling in fact that after all she had no wish to leave Ulverston House.

She had a feeling that Lady Adelaide would be extremely annoyed if she remained there so long, but if Orlena could manage to keep out of her way as she had done this past week or so, she hoped that she could prevent the much-acclaimed beauty from being too unpleasant.

"Leave everything in my hands," the Earl said, "and, Orlena, go on playing. I believe Mr. Greville is arranging tuition for you, but perhaps what you feel and what you say in your music is the best teacher you could have."

The Earl rose as he spoke and Orlena stared at him wide-eyed.

She had never imagined that he of all people would understand what her music meant to her, but there was no doubt that he did understand.

Because he was preparing to leave she too rose to her feet. He looked down at her and she thought there was a faint smile on his lips as he said:

"Try to enjoy yourself. As you grow older the disillusionment comes all too quickly."

He turned away from her as he spoke, not waiting for an answer.

Only when he left the room did she stand staring at the closed door, feeling that he had disturbed her emotionally although she could not understand why.

He was indeed disillusioned, she thought, that was obvious.

Something had made him cynical, something which, despite his rank and great possessions, had made him look at life with a boredom which showed itself all too clearly in the way he spoke.

Yet everything round him was so beautiful and so perfectly arranged that it was hard to believe any man could remain discontented.

'One day perhaps I shall learn why he is like that,' Orlena thought.

But she told herself she would be far too shy and it would sound far too inquisitive to ask the Countess. And she was absolutely certain that the Earl would never tell her about himself.

Yet she found herself thinking about him and when she went downstairs to the Salon she found it hard to concentrate on the book she had brought with her.

She had in fact been reading for only a short time when the door opened and Terry came in.

Orlena looked up excitedly.

She was always thrilled to see her brother and she thought as he advanced down the room towards her that he looked very different from the way he had during the dreary months at Weldon Park when he had had nothing to do but grumble.

He was dressed in the very height of fashion and not only appeared very handsome and attractive but his whole face was animated, and she knew by the light in his eyes that he had something important to tell her.

"Are you alone?" he asked.

"There is no-one hiding under the sofa as far as I am aware," Orlena replied laughingly.

Terry glanced towards the door.

"I want to talk to you and I do not want to be interrupted."

"As far as I know there is no likelihood of that," Orlena replied. "The Duchess has gone to a Reception and will not be back for hours."

Terry sat down on the sofa beside his sister and said:

"I want you to help me."

"Of course, you know I will do anything you want," Orlena replied. "What has happened?"

Terry lowered his voice.

"I want you to come with me this evening to Astley's Amphitheatre."

"A theatre?" Orlena exclaimed. "You know I would love that. What is the play?"

"It is not a play, it is a Circus," Terry replied.

"A Circus?" Orlena exclaimed.

"It is very well known," Terry said quickly. "It started over twenty-seven years ago and is now the one place in London where you can see really first-class equestrian displays."

"Of course I would like to come with you," Orlena said. "Is there anything secret about our going there?"

Terry made a grimace at her.

"I thought you would soon tumble to the fact that it is not really the sort of place to which I should take you. At least, I have the idea that His Lordship would disapprove, but then he disapproves of everything where you are concerned."

"Why particularly do you wish me to come with you?" Orlena asked.

She was quite well aware, knowing her brother, that what he was suggesting was not as straightforward as it might appear.

Terry hesitated.

"There is a girl involved," he said at length. "I want to take her out to supper after the show, but she has already promised somebody else, so the only thing to do is to make a foursome of it."

He paused, then added a little awkwardly:

"She suggested I might bring another female with me, but quite frankly, Orlena, I do not know one I could ask."

"But of course I will come with you," Orlena exclaimed. "Who is this girl?"

"She is fantastic!" Terry said enthusiastically. "When you see her ride you will realise that there has never been anyone like her, and her horse is incredible! It can read—at least that is the impression it gives as it picks out the letters of the alphabet."

"Are you telling me," Orlena asked incredulously, "that this girl is a performer in the Circus?"

"That is right," Terry said. "But she is very sweet and quite respectable. There is nothing wrong with her, but you know how stuffy the Earl and the Duchess would be if they learnt you were meeting her."

Orlena was silent for a moment and Terry said:

"Please come with me, Orlena. I really do not know anyone else to ask."

"Of course I will," Orlena replied. "There is no reason for us to tell lies, but we need not volunteer information."

"I agree," Terry smiled.

"I shall just tell Her Grace that I am going out to dinner with you and some friends," Orlena said. "She will make no objections, I am sure, and there is no reason for the Earl to know anything about it."

"No, of course not," Terry said in relief, "and as the show starts early, the sooner we get away from here, the better."

"What should I wear?" Orlena enquired.

"Oh, something rather quiet and simple," Terry replied. "We shall be going on to a Restaurant but not one which is considered fast or improper. All I want is to be able to talk to Jenny, and if you will keep the other member of the party amused it will make it easier."

"I will do my best," Orlena promised.

Everything worked out rather better than she had expected.

Terry wished to slip away before six o'clock and she found as she was leaving Ulverston House that the Duchess had not returned.

Orlena therefore left her a note explaining that Terry had asked her to go out to dinner and apologising for not being able to accompany her to a party given by the Duchess of Richmond.

"They will not miss me," she told herself confidently.

Terry collected her in a very smart closed carriage and they set off for the Amphitheatre, which Orlena learnt was in Westminster Bridge Road.

"Tell me about Miss Stevens," she said.

"I met her three nights ago at a party in Vauxhall Gardens," Terry replied, "and when I went to see the Circus I was astonished by her performance. I have never seen anything like it, Orlena!"

"And you enjoyed the other turns?"

"They were quite fantastic!"

Watching the riding displays later in the Amphitheatre, Orlena realised that Terry had not exaggerated.

She had never imagined that horses could be trained to give such exciting performances and she joined in the enthusiastic applause, understanding why Terry found it so fascinating.

She learnt from a pamphlet which listed the turns that the Amphitheatre had been opened in 1780.

The ex-Sergeant-Major Philip Astley had founded a riding school and because he was an outstanding rider, as were his wife, his son John, and his daughter Hannah, he had extended this superb horseback spectacle of trick-riding.

The Amphitheatre was rather primitive, as it had originally been a timber-yard.

There was a stage and in front of it a sawdust ring where the horses performed. There were a few private boxes but the seats in the rest of the building were of wood.

Terry had learnt that the original building had been burnt down and this one erected now was mostly of ships' masts and spars with a ceiling stretched on four poles.

But if the accommodation was amateurish, the turns were very professional. These included acrobatics and rope-vaulting, besides dancing dogs, and bears which stood upon their heads and were ridden by apes.

There were monkeys which turned head-over-heels with lighted candles in their paws and horses which stood on their hind legs and boxed with each other.

It was not difficult to know when Jenny Stevens appeared without looking at the programme.

Terry sat forward in the box and Orlena glancing at his face realised that he was entranced by the exquisite little figure who danced like a second Taglioni on the back of a white horse.

She was described in the programme as "a gauzy

and roseate dream" and Orlena did not think that it over-praised her.

She certainly looked young and lovely, and the horse galloping round while she pirouetted on its back roused the audience to a frenzy of excitement.

When Jenny had finished her riding display, a pianoforte was moved into the centre of the ring and the letters of the alphabet, large enough for everyone to see, were laid out in a row.

To soft music Jenny's horse proceeded to spell out words not only at the command of his mistress but also those which were shouted from the audience.

They were quite simple words, like "cat" and "dog," "bat" and "ball," but the horse faltered only once and chose a wrong letter.

"It is incredible!" Orlena exclaimed as Jenny rode off standing on her horse's back and blowing kisses to the crowd.

Terry got to his feet.

"Come on, Orlena!" he said. "We can go round now to Jenny's dressing-room."

The thought of it gave Orlena a feeling of excitement.

She had never thought she would go behind a stage and see the difference from the way it appeared at the front. The red curtains, bright lights, the attractively painted scenery, and the sparkling animation of the performers seemed very glamorous.

But behind it was a different story, with a jungle of ropes, wires, and nets, unpainted passages, the smell of animals, and a general barely lit gloom.

Terry led the way up the wooden staircase and at the top of it were rows of dressing-rooms, through the half-open doors of which Orlena could see the performers in various stages of undress.

Terry knocked on one closed door and they entered to find it small and incredibly untidy, but apparently empty, until a voice asked:

"Is that you, Terry?"

Orlena realised that Jenny Stevens was changing behind a screen.

"It is!" Terry replied. "And I have brought my sister with me. She is supping with us tonight."

"I thought you'd find a girl if you tried hard enough!" came the laughing reply.

A second later the screen was pushed to one side and Jenny Stevens appeared.

She was not as young as she had seemed from the front of the house, but Orlena thought she was certainly very pretty with fair hair that was suspiciously golden and laughing blue eyes with heavily mascaraed lashes.

She had a pouting red mouth which when she smiled showed two rows of pearly white teeth.

Jenny Stevens held out her hand.

"I don't know what you'll think of this untidy room," she said, "but my dresser's ill, and if you want a drink, Terry, you'll have to fetch yourself one."

"I will wait until we have supper," Terry answered. "Where is the fourth member of the party?"

"He'll be along," Jenny answered. "He was in a box on the other side of the house from you, and I dare say he's waiting to see the waltzing ponies."

"I think the turns are marvellous!" Orlena enthused. "However did you teach your horse to read in that clever manner?"

"He wasn't very clever tonight," Jenny said sharply. "Pat, who plays the piano for me, was drunk again. That's the third time this week! He made Snowball make a mistake, as I expect you saw. If he does it again I've told him I'll find someone else!"

"You mean your horse chooses the letters by music?" Orlena asked.

"That's right," Jenny said. "It's the notes which tell him which letter to choose."

"I think it was the cleverest trick I have ever seen," Orlena said, and Jenny smiled at her.

"I don't know what I'd do without Snowball. My father trained him. When I have a nightmare it's that Snowball's dead and I've got to train another horse. Quite frankly, I don't know how I'd start about it."

"There is plenty of life left in Snowball," Terry said lightly.

"I hope you're right," Jenny replied seriously.

A moment later she was laughing gaily and introducing the fourth member of their party, who had just entered the dressing-room.

They went to a Restaurant which, while Orlena found it rather fascinating, she could not help thinking would not have obtained the approval of the Earl.

There were a lot of diners who belonged to the stage and all seemed to be friends of Jenny, who was waving and blowing kisses to them all through the meal.

The food was good if rather solidly English, but Terry and Lord Westover, who was the other guest, both pronounced the wine quite palatable.

Because Orlena knew what Terry expected of her she tried to hold Lord Westover's attention and found it surprisingly easy.

A man of perhaps twenty-five, as Orlena learnt by the end of the evening, he had only recently inherited his title, but his father had left him little else.

"I have come to London to try to make my fortune," he said frankly.

"How do you intend to do that?" Orlena enquired.

He shrugged his shoulders.

"I expect I shall have to marry an heiress," he said. "She is sure to be pock-marked and have a squint, but there is no other way by which I can live in comfort."

Orlena did not say anything and she realised that he had no idea that she was in fact an heiress. She found it amusing to remain anonymous and talk to him about his aspirations.

"Surely there is something better you can do than marry someone with whom you are not in love, simply because she has money?"

"What alternative is there?" he enquired. "I could throw away the pittance I have left by playing cards or putting it on a horse, but you know as well as I do that money makes money and those who have none always lose."

"I agree that that would be very stupid," Orlena said. "I suppose it would be impossible for you to find employment of some sort?"

"What can I do?" he enquired. "To suggest anything so reprehensible as being in trade would be to bar me from the few Clubs to which I can still afford to belong."

"It seems a foolish way of living," Orlena said. "I think men should be occupied either in making money if they need it, or in social reform through Politics if they do not."

Lord Westover laughed.

"You are frightening me, Miss Weldon, and after all what does your brother do except make eyes at every pretty girl?"

His eyes were twinkling as she realised that Terry was completely monopolising Jenny Stevens.

"I am not complaining," he added quickly. "I am perfectly content, Miss Weldon. But Jenny had promised to dine with me."

"Shall I try to take my brother away?" Orlena asked.

"Certainly not. I want you to go on talking to me, and inspiring me."

"Can I do that?" Orlena asked.

"Very easily," he replied.

She realised by the end of the evening that he admired and was attracted by her but he still had no idea that she was an heiress.

He offered to pay half the bill when it was time for them to leave the Restaurant.

"This is Terry's party," Orlena said firmly, kicking her brother under the table.

"As we barged in on your tête-á-tête," Terry said, taking the hint, "I insist on being your host. You can return the compliment another time."

Orlena thought Lord Westover was relieved and she could understand his feelings when she glanced at the bill. It came to quite a lot of money, owing to the amount of expensive drink the two gentlemen had consumed.

"Jenny and I are going to Vauxhall Gardens," Terry said almost defiantly as they rose to leave the Restaurant. "I am sure, Orlena, you would wish to go home."

"Yes, of course," Orlena agreed meekly, knowing that that was what Terry expected of her.

"I too will say good-night," Lord Westover said, "and I do not mind telling you, Weldon, I think you have been a bit high-handed over this evening."

Terry laughed and Orlena realised he had intended from the very first to have Jenny Stevens to himself.

"Where are you staying?" Lord Westover asked.

"In Park Lane," Orlena replied.

He raised his eye-brows, then he said:

"It seems ridiculous for everyone to drive all that way when Vauxhall Gardens is not far from here. Would you trust me to take you home alone?"

"But of course," Orlena replied.

Lord Westover arranged it with Terry, who was not prepared to argue, and Orlena found herself driving with Lord Westover in a hackney-carriage.

"You are very attractive," he said after a moment. "Will you allow me to see you again?"

"But of course," Orlena replied. "The only difficulty is that we are staying in my Guardian's house and I have very little say as to what I can or cannot do."

"Who is your Guardian?" Lord Westover asked.

"The Earl of Ulverston."

She realised in the darkness of the carriage that he was staring at her in astonishment. Then he said:

"They were saying in the Club that Ulverston had introduced an extremely pretty heiress into the Social World. Can she possibly be you?"

"I am afraid it must be."

"Good God! And you let me talk about myself —telling you what I was planning to do?"

"There is no harm in that," Orlena replied, "and I have already told you that I think it is a mistake to try to solve your problems by marriage."

"You make it impossible for me now to say what I had intended to," Lord Westover said. "You will never believe that I was thinking about you and not about your money."

"I think I would always know if a man is being sincere or not," Orlena replied. "So please, do not think of me as an heiress . . . and I have enjoyed this evening very much."

"But you think it is unlikely that it is something we will repeat?" Lord Westover asked.

Orlena made a little helpless gesture with her hand.

"I do not know," she answered. "It is honestly very difficult for me."

"There is no reason to say any more," Lord Westover said. "I know perfectly well the reception I should get from His Lordship if I so much as tried to cross the threshold of Ulverston House."

Orlena did not know what to say and because she felt embarrassed she was glad when the carriage reached Park Lane and turned in between the two supercilious griffons.

"Thank you very much for bringing me home," she said politely.

Lord Westover took her hand in his and kissed it.

"You are everything a man could look for and

admire," he said, "and be damned to your money!
You have spoilt me for any other heiress!"

Orlena laughed a little self-consciously, and when
she stepped out at Ulverston House, Lord Westover
held her hand for longer than was necessary despite
the fact that there were two footmen in attendance
at the front door.

"I shall try to see you again," he said in a low
voice which only she could hear. "Make no mistake
about that, although I realise it will not be easy."

"Thank you for bringing me home," Orlena said
again.

Then she was free of him and walked into the
house without looking back.

She moved towards the staircase and was just
about to put her foot on the first step when she heard
someone speak her name.

There was no mistaking the authoritative drawl
and she turned round quickly to see the Earl standing in the doorway of the Salon.

She waited and he said:

"Will you come in here?"

Before she responded, she had an uncomfortable
feeling that he was about to find fault, but since she
could hardly refuse to do as he asked she walked
across the Hall and entered the Salon.

He shut the door behind her and she moved towards the fireplace, feeling uncomfortably aware that
there was no-one else in the room and she and the
Earl were alone.

When she reached the fire she bent down to put
her hands out towards the flames, realising that she
felt cold and not certain if it was from the chill wind
outside or because she was feeling nervous.

"Who brought you home?" the Earl demanded.

"Lord Westover."

"Alone?"

"Yes."

"Why? Where is the Duchess?"

"I did not go out with the Duchess tonight," Orlena answered. "Terry wanted me to dine with him."

"And where is your brother now?"

"He wished to visit Vauxhall Gardens and he sent me home."

"I should hope so," the Earl said. "Vauxhall Gardens is not a proper place for a young girl to be seen in at night. Why did he not bring you back himself?"

Orlena thought quickly that the Earl would certainly not be pleased if he knew where in fact she had spent the evening, so she said quickly:

"Lord Westover was coming this way and he offered to be my escort."

"I am sure he did!" the Earl said grimly. "I presume you know he is a fortune-hunter?"

"Yes, he told me so," Orlena answered.

She thought with satisfaction that her reply had surprised the Earl.

She glanced at him now and saw that he was looking more resplendent than usual and there were two diamond-encrusted decorations pinned to his evening-coat. She guessed he had been dining at Carlton House with the Prince of Wales.

"It seems extraordinary to me," the Earl said, and now there was no doubt that his tone was scathing, "that while I provide you with one of the most distinguished Chaperons in London you still contrive to behave in an extremely foolish manner."

Orlena bent her head. She felt very like a school-child being rebuked by the Mistress.

"It is not correct," the Earl continued, "for a young girl to drive alone at night with a man, as you must be aware. Or had Lord Westover some special attraction for you and you wish to flaunt the conventions where he is concerned?"

"I have . . . no desire to . . . do that."

"You seem to get yourself into situations which,

if known, would certainly react unfavourably on your reputation."

"I am ... sorry," Orlena murmured.

She sat down on the hearth-rug in front of the fire and now the velvet cloak she had worn to go to the Amphitheatre slipped from her shoulders and the firelight shone on her white neck and arms.

There was something young and defenceless in her bent head and downcast eyes.

"Are you in love with this man?"

The question was sharp and it seemed to Orlena to echo round the room.

She turned her face to look at the Earl in surprise.

"No, of course not! I met him for the first time this evening."

"And yet you became intimate enough for him to tell you that he was looking for an heiress?"

"He did not know who I was. It was only when I told him where I was staying that he had any idea that I might have money of my own."

"How very convenient for him!" the Earl sneered.

"It is the truth!" Orlena retorted.

"But you are already enamoured of him!"

"Nothing of the sort!" Orlena replied. "He is a nice young man and I felt very sorry for him because he is poor. I have been poor too. Anyway, I told him it would be very difficult for us to meet again."

"You want to meet him again?"

"Not particularly," Orlena answered.

She gave a little sigh of exasperation.

"You are trying to make a mountain out of a mole-hill, you are twisting something I have done, perhaps stupidly, and giving it much more importance than it actually has."

The Earl did not speak and after a moment she said:

"I told your mother I should make mistakes and

make you angry. That is why it would be better if Terry and I lived on our own."

"So that you can make a thousand more?" the Earl asked scornfully.

"Why should it worry you?" she asked. "I know you are our Guardian, but it cannot really matter to you one way or the other what I do. I am just a 'Miss Nobody from Nowhere' who has been forced upon you against your will. Forget about me, My Lord; I do not suppose I shall come to any real harm."

"I would not be too sure about that!" the Earl replied. "I have rescued you once, if you remember, from an unpleasant situation. I might not be there to rescue you another time."

Orlena felt the colour rise in her cheeks as she remembered all too vividly what had happened after he had rescued her.

"You are very lovely, Orlena!" he said in a voice she had not heard him use before. "It is very difficult for anyone as lovely as you not to become embroiled in situations they might afterwards regret."

Because for once he was not lecturing or sneering at her, Orlena looked at him in surprise.

She met his eyes and somehow they seemed to hold her spellbound.

The strange feeling she had known before when he kissed her seemed to move into her throat and she felt herself tremble.

"You must try to be more careful," the Earl said as if he spoke to a child.

"I will . . . try," Orlena said.

It was impossible to look away from him and she had a sudden longing to move nearer still.

He had revived the wonder and rapture she had known when he first kissed her.

Then because she was shy and nervous she forced herself to rise to her feet.

"I think I should . . . go to bed . . . My Lord."

He did not answer and she bent down to pick up her cloak from where it lay on the floor.

She realised he had not risen as she had and was still sitting in the chair, leaning back, his eyes on her face.

"I ... I am ... sorry I am so ... foolish," she said almost in a whisper.

Then she turned and ran away from him without looking back.

Chapter Five

Orlena driving back towards Park Lane said to the maid who accompanied her:

"I hope you found it interesting, Nicholls. I had no idea that Westminster Abbey embodied so much history."

"Nor had I, Miss," Nicholls replied.

She was a middle-aged woman who was the head housemaid at Ulverston House.

It was Mr. Greville who had arranged that when Orlena wished to go shopping or to visit the sights of London she should be accompanied by Nicholls.

She certainly looked the part, Orlena thought, of a respectable and rather disapproving Abigail.

But on closer acquaintance she found that Nicholls was an extremely nice woman who had come from the country and who disapproved of what she called the "goings on" in London.

Now as they neared Ulverston House Orlena said in a low voice:

"You did not tell anyone of what happened a fortnight ago at St. James's Church, or that we went there again last week?"

"No, Miss, of course not," Nicholls replied. "You asked me not to say anything and I would not break my word."

She paused, then she said:

"Most of them in the house are not interested in anything but gossip, an ignorant lot compared to the staff in His Lordship's house in the country."

Orlena smiled.

She had already heard Nicholls's conviction that everything in the country was vastly superior to what was to be found in London.

As the carriage passed the griffons at the gates she said:

"Thank you, Nicholls, for coming with me. I hope we shall be able to visit some more sights. I want to see everything before I leave London."

"It's a pleasure to go with you, Miss," Nicholls said, and Orlena knew she meant it.

She had in fact, with Nicholls to escort her, visited the Tower of London, St. Paul's Cathedral, and Kew Gardens.

No-one else was interested in seeing the sights and Orlena was determined that she would not return to Weldon Park until she had seen everything which the guide-books told her were of importance.

It was incredible to think that she had been at Ulverston House for nearly six weeks and in a fortnight's time the London Season would be coming to an end.

She had enjoyed herself, she thought, but it still seemed extraordinary how little she had seen of the Earl and how easily she had been able to avoid coming into contact with Lady Adelaide.

She imagined they were together, but she did not know.

All she was aware of was that she looked forward to the evenings when she saw the Earl at the head of the dining-table or saw him moving amongst his guests with that bored, cynical expression on his face.

He nevertheless out-topped in magnificence every other man present.

He had walked into the Library unexpectedly a fortnight ago when she had been trying to decide which of his books she would read next.

He was wearing riding-clothes and was obviously just about to leave the house for the Park.

"I was told you were here, Orlena," he said.

"I am choosing one of your books," she smiled. "I hope you do not mind."

"I am delighted!" the Earl replied. "I sometimes find it difficult to keep up with all the purchases Greville makes on my behalf."

Orlena smiled.

"I am only too willing to make up for your deficiencies, My Lord."

"So I hear," he said, "but as you well know, I think you should be dancing rather than wearing your eyes out with small print."

Orlena laughed again.

"You sound exactly like my old Nanny," she said. "She always talked as if my eyes were a pair of shoes and I was wearing them down at the heels!"

The Earl looked amused, then said:

"By the way, Orlena, I have had a letter from your Solicitors in Yorkshire, asking if you have any knowledge of where your father kept documents appertaining to the Estate."

"Do you mean leases and papers like that?" Orlena enquired.

"I imagine so," the Earl replied casually.

"Then if they are not in his desk," Orlena said, "there is what was always known as the 'secret cupboard' in his bed-room. When it is closed it looks like part of the panelling. They can find the opening by pressing a large carved Tudor rose nearest to the top of the mantelshelf."

"I will tell Mr. Thorogood, if that is his name," the Earl said.

"There is nothing of importance in the cupboard,"

Orlena told him. "I looked there just before we left."

"Are you sure?" the Earl asked.

"Quite sure," Orlena replied. "It is where Papa always kept any jewellery Mama and I owned. When I collected a brooch and a bracelet, which I have with me, I noticed that the shelves were practically empty."

"Thank you, Orlena," the Earl said.

He walked towards the door, then turned back to say:

"It is a lovely day and I think if you are intent on reading you should do so in the garden."

"Since you are so concerned about my health, My Lord," Orlena replied, "I will do what you tell me to do."

"That will be a change!" the Earl retorted, and left her.

Orlena remembered feeling a little wistful when he had gone because although he rode every day he never asked her to accompany him.

She did in fact ride in the Park occasionally with Terry, and she knew she had only to ask Mr. Greville and he would send a groom to accompany her. But she would have liked above everything else to ride with the Earl.

Then she told herself that it was obvious that he could not be seen with her when he in fact belonged to Lady Adelaide.

Perhaps they rode together, Orlena was not sure, but she knew that the Earl took Lady Adelaide driving in his high-perch Phaeton and she had envied the beauty the experience.

The carriage drew up at the front door and the footmen hurried down the steps to roll out the red carpet and open the door for Orlena to alight.

She smiled her thanks, knowing them all well by now. She had been told by Nicholls that the majority of them came from the Earl's Estate in the country, where their fathers and grandfathers had served the family for generations.

As she entered the house the Butler came forward to say:

"His Lordship asks that you go to the Library immediately on your return."

Orlena's heart gave a little jump.

It was a summons that had not come for some time and she wondered why the Earl wished to see her.

"Shall I take your bonnet, Miss?" Nicholls asked.

"Yes, Nicholls, that is a good idea. I shall not want my reticule either."

She handed the satin bag which hung from her wrist to the maid, then took off her high-crowned bonnet.

It was trimmed with a wreath of cornflowers and poppies which matched the ribbons which crossed under her breast and tied behind her straight gown in long streamers which reached the floor.

Orlena tidied her hair and, realising that she was looking her best, followed the Butler down the corridor to the Library.

He opened the door.

"Miss Weldon, M'Lord!" he announced.

The Earl was sitting at his desk and as Orlena looked at him she realised in consternation and with a constriction of her heart that the Earl was scowling and looked in fact extremely angry.

He did not rise, but his eyes, dark and penetrating, were on her face as she walked towards him, aware of a feeling of nervousness and wondering frantically what had upset him.

When she reached the desk she stood in front of him and he said sharply in a tone which made her jump:

"I want an explanation of this!"

He pointed as he spoke to a paper which lay on the desk.

"What is it?" Orlena asked, feeling because she was frightened that her eyes could not focus on what was in front of him.

"It is a statement from your Bank," the Earl replied, "and I would like an explanation, Orlena, as to why on the 15th of the month and again on the 20th you drew out the sum of five hundred pounds."

Orlena did not speak and the Earl said scathingly and contemptuously in a tone she had heard from him before:

"I want the name, Orlena, of the young fortune-hunter to whom you are being so generous."

"I . . . it is nothing like . . . that," she said, finding it difficult to speak.

"Do not lie!" the Earl said furiously. "I am not a fool, although I was prepared to believe you when you told me you had no wish to go to parties or Balls, but preferred to stay at home."

He thumped with his clenched hand on the desk as he went on:

"How could I have been so blind or so idiotic as to trust your word? But I thought you were different from other women, only to find I am mistaken."

"But . . . I am not . . ." Orlena tried to say.

He interrupted her before the words had passed her lips, storming furiously:

"You will tell me the name of this man to whom you have not only given your money but doubtless your lips, as you gave them to me, and maybe also your body!"

Orlena stiffened and now her temper, which was very seldom roused, made her face the Earl with her eyes blazing.

"How dare you speak to me like that!" she said. "How dare you suggest such a thing! There is no man such as you are insinuating!"

The Earl rose to his feet.

"I am prepared to believe only the evidence of
my own eyes," he said. "Five hundred pounds! It is
a considerable sum, Orlena, on the 15th and again on
the 20th. Will you tell me the recipient's name, or
have I to shake it out of you?"

He seemed to tower above her but for once she
was not afraid, only angry.

"Your suspicions are quite unfounded, My Lord,"
she said, "and before I give you an explanation
I would point out that it is my own money I am
spending. Even as my Guardian you have no right
to interfere."

"I have every right," the Earl said angrily, "and
I will not allow you to be bled white by some charlatan with whom doubtless you think yourself enamoured."

"There is no charlatan," Orlena replied, "and
your suspicions are so insulting that I have no wish
to explain my actions to you."

"Nevertheless, you will explain them!"

The Earl was speaking so violently and with so
much fury in his voice that, incensed though she was,
Orlena felt forced to obey him and tell him what he
wished to know.

"Very well, My Lord, I will tell you why I spent
the money," she said, and her voice was still angry,
her eyes defiant.

"On May 15th, early in the morning I went with
Nicholls to visit St. James's Church in Westminster."

The Earl raised his eye-brows and she thought
he looked disbelieving as she went on furiously:

"If you are interested, I went into the Church
because I wished to say a prayer of gratitude and
thanks for the kindness I have received since I came
to London from both your mother and Your Lordship.
I do not suppose you will understand, but that is
what I desired to do."

There was still a look of cynical disbelief in the Earl's expression and Orlena continued:

"When I entered the Church-yard I saw what appeared to be a bundle lying on the path. When I looked closer I found it was a child of about three who appeared to be dead. It was so thin, so emaciated, that it seemed impossible there could be any life in it."

Orlena paused a moment, remembering how the child's appearance had shocked her. Then she went on:

"I took it into the Church and found the Vicar. It was then I learnt that it was nothing unusual for him to find a dozen or more children in the vicinity of St. James's, dead in the streets or laid in the Church-yard."

Orlena's voice was as scathing as the Earl's had been as she went on:

"Members of the Nobility like yourself obviously fail to notice what is happening in London and they are not interested in the reports on the suffering of children which the Vicar showed me."

Orlena gave a deep sigh before she said:

"Do you know that half the children in the Workhouse at St. Martin's-in-the-Fields die every year? And the same applies to the Workhouse belonging to St. George's, Hanover Square, where the *Beau Monde* are married."

There was a throb in her voice as she said:

"No-one cares, and although apparently there have been a certain number of speeches made in Parliament about the subject, I doubt if Your Lordship has bothered to listen to them."

The Earl did not speak and Orlena moved away from the desk to stand looking blindly into the garden while the tears were gathering in her eyes.

"The Parish of St. James's is the only one which has tried to do anything," she continued. "They have

billeted the Parish children not in Workhouses but in
carefully selected cottages on Wimbledon Common."

Before she went on, she paused to try to control
her voice:

"A Nurse is allowed three shillings per week for
each of the five or six children entrusted to her, and
she is paid a bonus if the children keep in good
health."

With an effort Orlena prevented the tears in her
eyes from falling as she said:

"Need I say that because there is so little money
only comparatively few children can be looked after
in this way? I gave the Vicar five hundred pounds,
then when I came back here I thought I had been
. . . mean and cheese-paring . . . like Papa."

She made a gesture with her hands.

"I had only to look at this house and its contents
to realise that hundreds—perhaps a thousand—of
children's lives could be saved on what is expended
on pictures, furniture, food, and servants. So because
I was so ashamed of having so much when they have
so . . . little, I went back the following week and . . .
gave the Vicar another . . . five hundred pounds."

Orlena's voice died away and there was silence
until the Earl said quietly and in a very different
tone:

"Forgive me, Orlena."

There was a pause before she answered him, her
voice almost indistinct:

"I can never . . . forgive you for what you . . .
thought."

She turned round and now he could see the tears
running down her cheeks.

"When you . . . kissed me," she said incoherently,
"it was . . . everything that was . . . beautiful and . . .
perfect. It was like . . . music . . . it was . . . glorious and
good. But now you have made it seem wrong and . . .
horrible, and I . . . hate you!"

It was impossible through her tears to see the Earl's face, and because she could no longer control the emotions which shook her whole body she turned and ran from the room.

She went along the passage and up the stairs to her bed-room, locking the door and flinging herself down on the bed to cry as if her heart were breaking.

She cried for a long time. Then gradually, with her breath coming fitfully between her lips, she could think coherently of how the Earl had insulted her and what he believed her to have done.

"How could he?" she asked herself.

Ever since their first meeting he had found her badly behaved and reprehensible.

But that he would really suppose that she had a lover to whom she was giving money, a man she was ashamed to acknowledge publicly, was so degrading that Orlena felt as if she were humiliated into the dust.

"I wanted him to like and admire me."

She remembered how rapturous and wonderful his kiss for her had been, while to him it had meant only something cheap and promiscuous.

The tears began to flow again as she thought how magnificent the Earl always looked, and how despite the fact that she was frightened of him she admired him and until now had trusted him.

"I wanted him to like me," she told herself again, then was still.

Quite suddenly she realised why she was so distressed at what he had thought, why because he was angry the world seemed to have come to an end.

She fought against the conviction that was slowly forcing itself into her mind.

"It is not true! It cannot be true!" she whispered.

But even as she protested she knew that it was irrefutably true. She loved the Earl!

"How can I possibly do anything so absurd?" she tried to argue. "He has nothing but contempt for me. He is to marry the beautiful Lady Adelaide. He is concerned that I shall not make a fool of myself only because he is my Guardian. I am nothing but a nuisance, a tiresome girl who is always making mistakes and doing the wrong things."

She knew all the arguments, but she also knew that the reason why her heart had beat more quickly when she went to the Library was that the Earl wanted to see her.

She had been so deeply and abjectly distressed by his accusations simply because it was he who had made them.

Had anyone else made such insulting suggestions, when she had a perfectly reasonable explanation, it would indeed have made her angry; but it would not have been the same devastating, soul-destroying misery which she felt now.

"I love him! I love him!" she cried into her damp pillow, and knew that nothing could be more hopeless, nothing more foolish.

She was startled by a knock on the door.

"Who is it?" she asked.

"It is Nicholls, Miss."

With an effort Orlena rose from the bed and unlocked the door.

As Nicholls entered she turned away so that the maid would not see her tear-stained face.

"There's a note from His Lordship for you, Miss."

Orlena felt herself tremble. Then with an eagerness she could not control, she put out her hand to take the note from the silver salver on which Nicholls presented it.

She walked over to the window to stand with her back to the room as she opened the thick vellum envelope on which her name was inscribed in His Lordship's strong, distinctive hand-writing.

Inside there was a sheet of crested writing-paper on which there was written one line:

"*I apologise very humbly.*"

Orlena stared at it and realised that something else had been enclosed in the envelope.

She looked at it and saw that it was some pages torn from a pamphlet entitled *An Act for the Better Regulation of Poor Parish Children.*

Printed below was the report of a Committee set up to enquire into the problem.

It recommended that children under six years of age should be sent to the country "not less than three miles off," to be boarded there at the cost of their respective Parishes. The report continued:

> If this is not possible, owing to the number of children concerned, orphanages should be erected on the lines of the three which have proved so successful on the Ulverston Estates in Kent. It has been learnt that in these three Homes there have been no deaths for the last two years. The Inspectors report that all the children are in good health and there has been little call for medical attention.

Orlena read the torn-out pages through for the second time and felt ashamed of the manner in which she had attacked the Earl.

He deserved it, she thought; and yet he had an explanation, as she had, and it was impossible for her not to accept his apology.

Because she loved him, and because she longed to unsay the bitter words with which she had stormed at him, she went at once to the *Secretaire* which stood in the corner of the bed-room.

Opening it, she took out a piece of writing-paper and did not consider what she should say but wrote what came straight into her head:

I am Sorry I was Rude. I am Sorry too that
I Misjudged Your Lordship. Please forgive
Me and think a little more Kindly of Your
most Humble and Penetential Ward,
                                        Orlena.

She put the writing-paper into an envelope, addressed it to the Earl, then realised that Nicholls was
still in the room tidying her gowns in the wardrobe.

"Is His Lordship downstairs?" she asked.

"No, Miss," Nicholls replied, "after he had given
James the note for me to bring to you, His Lordship
went riding. I saw him ride down the drive with my
own eyes."

He would be back for luncheon, Orlena thought,
and he must receive her apology before they met.

She thought there was to be a luncheon-party,
although she was not sure. But she felt she could not
see him before he knew that she was sorry for the
manner in which she had raged at him.

Without giving any instructions to Nicholls, she
ran down the stairs and went to the Library.

She put the note she carried in her hand on the
Earl's desk, propping it against the ink-pot.

On the open blotter she saw the statement from
the Bank which had made him so suspicious and angry.

She took a glance at it and realised that she had
in fact spent a great deal of money since she came
to London.

The Earl had told both her and Terry immediately after their arrival that they could draw up to
two thousand pounds.

Orlena saw now that with the bills she had paid
for her clothes and the thousand pounds she had
given to St. James's Church she had in fact only a
few hundred still in hand.

"I shall have to be more economical," she told
herself with a little smile.

Inadvertently she moved the Bank-statement and saw that lying beneath it was a letter headed with the names "Thorogood, Harrow and Chesnet."

They would be writing to His Lordship, she thought, about the Estate, and she wondered why he had not told her what they had said. She hoped the Solicitors were not making any alterations to the house without first consulting Terry.

Without really thinking what she was doing, she picked up the letter and saw that it was signed by Mr. Thorogood.

It was addressed: "To the Right Honourable Earl of Ulverston."

My Lord:

It is with the deepest regret and consternation that I write to inform you that my firm, having made an extremely thorough investigation of the Deed Boxes deposited by the late Sir Hamish Weldon in the Bank of York, are unable to discover any of the Bearer Bonds which constitute the principal part of Sir Hamish's Estate.

These, following our client's instructions, had been placed by ourselves for safekeeping in the vaults of the Bank. We have just discovered that a week before he died Sir Hamish, without informing us, removed the Bonds while leaving the boxes in which they were housed intact.

A most thorough search has been made of Weldon Park but there is no sign whatsoever of these documents. I therefore beg you, My Lord, to communicate immediately with the Beneficiaries of the Estate, Sir Terence Weldon and Miss Orlena Weldon, and inform them that the information we conveyed to them concerning their inheritance was incorrect and they are in fact in debt to this firm for quite a considerable sum.

I and my partners can only ask Your Lordship's indulgence and understanding as to how this mistake arose, and express our very deep regret both to Your Lordship and to the two beneficiaries, who are Your Lordship's Wards.

We will continue to make every investigation and search for the missing Bonds, but we are in fact completely baffled as to how the late Sir Hamish could have disposed of them.

I remain,
                Your Lordship's most humble and
                        obedient servant,
                                Adolphus Thorogood.

Orlena stood as if turned to stone before she read and reread the letter again and again.

She could hardly credit that what it said was true, and yet there it was in front of her in black and white, and now the full horror of what it conveyed swept over her.

She and Terry were not only penniless as they had been before, but were also in debt to their Solicitors in Yorkshire and frighteningly under an obligation to repay the Earl for all he had expended on them.

It might be easier for Terry, she thought, because at least he had something to sell—his horses might even fetch more than he had given for them. But she had only her expensive clothes, which second-hand were worth nothing.

What was more, she owed the Earl a thousand pounds! It was his money she had given away so generously without consulting him.

She felt almost as if she must faint as the implication of what she read swept over her. Then she laid the letter down on the desk and walked slowly, very slowly, from the Library upstairs to her bed-room.

There was no-one there and she knew that the servants ate at noon and that Nicholls would have gone to the Housekeeper's room for her meal.

Orlena went to the *Secretaire* and wrote a letter to Terry.

She told him to demand to see the letter from Mr. Thorogood. Then she went on:

> You can Repay some of the Money You have spent, at any rate in part, and I am Determined that Somehow, however Long it takes Me, I will pay His Lordship back. It will take Time, but I will Manage it.
>
> I am going Away to find employment Somehow . . . Somewhere. Do not let His Lordship try to find Me. I do not wish for His or anyone's Charity.
>
> Please go to Weldon Park as soon as You can.
>
> My love,
> Orlena.

She addressed the letter to her brother, then hastily began to pack.

There were a number of gown-boxes in the wardrobe in which Orlena's gowns had been delivered from Bond Street.

She filled them all, and pushed some of her new bonnets into the round cardboard boxes which were embellished with the name of the most expensive Milliners in London.

It was impossible for her to get everything in, but she packed what she could, knowing that she would never be able to buy another gown, a pair of shoes, or even a nightgown, until she had paid back some of the money she owed the Earl.

She put on a bonnet and picked up a silk taffeta cloak which had been extremely expensive and put it on over her thin muslin gown.

She looked in her reticule and found that she had five sovereigns left of the money which Mr. Greville had advanced her to go shopping.

'That should last me some time if I am careful,' she thought.

At the same time, she felt a little stab of fear because she was stepping out into the unknown.

Then she told herself that anything was better than having to face the Earl, the Duchess, and perhaps Lady Adelaide, and then return to Yorkshire feeling as humble as she had when she first arrived in London.

A plan of what she should do was beginning to form in her mind.

Keeping an eye on the clock for fear that Nicholls might appear or that luncheon should be ready in the Dining-Room, she ran to the top of the stairs and called one of the footmen who were on duty in the Hall.

It was James, the red-headed one who had come from the country.

"I want you to bring the boxes from my room downstairs," Orlena said, "and call me a hackney-carriage."

"A hackney-carriage, Miss?" James exclaimed in surprise.

"Yes," Orlena answered. "I have to hurry to Bond Street with some gowns and it will take longer if we order His Lordship's horses from the stable."

"It wouldn't take more 'n five minutes, Miss."

"I want a hackney-carriage, James," Orlena said firmly.

She hurried down the stairs and he followed her a few moments later, carrying her boxes.

He set them down in the Hall and went out into

Park Lane to return almost immediately with a dilapidated-looking carriage drawn by a tired and obviously under-fed horse.

Orlena stepped into it and it seemed to her that James took an incredibly long time to set the boxes on the seat opposite her.

"What number in Bond Street, Miss?" he asked as he closed the carriage door.

"Twenty-two," Orlena said at random.

James gave the order to the coachman and they drove off, Orlena looking frantically towards the Park for fear that she might see the Earl returning from his ride.

As soon as they were out of the gates of Ulverston House she shouted to the driver:

"Go to Astley's Amphitheatre in Westminster Bridge Road!"

"Oi thought ye says Bond Street," the cabby replied surlily.

"I have changed my mind. You know the Amphitheatre, I suppose?"

"Oi knows it," the cabby replied.

"Then take me there as quickly as possible."

The cabman groaned but she supposed he would do as she asked, and she sat back, her brain racing as she tried to plan sensibly and quietly what she should do when she reached the Amphitheatre.

She had often thought of Jenny Stevens since she had met her that night with Terry; but when she had asked her brother about her a week or so later he had shrugged his shoulders and answered:

"I have not seen her lately."

"Oh, Terry, why not?"

He had given her one of his mischievous smiles.

"I found someone more attractive!"

"Oh, Terry! But she was so nice!"

"So is the dancer I am taking out to supper to-night."

"A dancer from the Amphitheatre?"

"Good God, no! Yvette dances at Covent Garden. She is what is known as one of the Opera Dancers and is the prettiest, most fascinating little creature you could possibly imagine!"

Terry had gone into eulogies over his new fancy. While Orlena had listened sympathetically, she could not help remembering how attractive Jenny Stevens had been and how cleverly her horse had picked out the alphabet.

Jenny had come to her mind now because Orlena knew the only possible way she could earn any money was by playing the piano.

Even the Earl had thought her talented, and she thought perhaps if there was not a place for her in the Amphitheatre, which she very much doubted, Jenny might know of other places where a pianist might be welcomed, even though she was a woman.

Orlena was a little vague about how she could manage to find work in such a capacity, but she thought it must be possible, and who was better able to help her than Jenny?

She only hoped as she neared the Amphitheatre that the dancer would not be annoyed because Terry was no longer interested in her.

Then she thought that, seeing how fascinating she was, there would be heaps of men like Lord Westover who would be only too pleased to take her out to supper and pay her compliments.

"It is really a blessing that Terry no longer sees her," Orlena told herself. "If he did, I am quite sure he would forbid me to ask Jenny for help, and like the Earl he would certainly disapprove of my trying to earn my own living."

She knew she would not have felt so horrified at the amount she owed if it had not been for the thousand pounds she had given away without consulting him.

Even if it had not been wasted, as he suspected, on a fortune-hunter, it was still a very large sum of money to have expended without advice.

She knew that the reports on his own Orphanages were not only an answer to the accusations she had made about his not caring for the dying children, but also showed her how foolishly impetuous she had been.

'I should have consulted someone before giving away such a large sum without considering it very carefully,' she thought.

She understood that the Earl and everyone else would think her both foolish and childishly irresponsible.

'Everything I do is wrong!' she thought despondently.

Then as the carriage plodded on she was sure that the Earl would now wash his hands of her completely and would no longer concern himself with her behaviour.

There would be no point in being a Guardian to someone who had no money, and she wished that some magic wand would put the clock back so that she and Terry should not have had their hopes unnecessarily raised by their father's will.

"It is so like Papa to disappoint and confound us at the very last moment," she told herself.

She knew how bitterly Terry would resent having to skimp and save as they had done before. It would be even worse now, because for nearly six weeks they had thought themselves rich and the heirs to a great fortune.

'At least we have had the experience,' she thought, and realised it was very cold comfort.

The carriage neared Astley's Amphitheatre. Orlena saw that it was a rather shabby, unprepossessing building and thought that in the daylight it seemed very different from its appearance at night.

It adjoined the main road with some fields and wasteland behind it in which a number of the horses and ponies were grazing.

The coachman turned from the box to shout:

"T'ain't open yet, Lidy!"

"I know that," Orlena replied. "There must be a side door where the performers enter the building."

The coachman drove her to a small, unpretentious entrance which had double doors wide enough to admit large animals and carriages.

There was a horse being led through one door as the hackney-carriage drew up.

"Will you wait for me?" Orlena asked the cabby.

"Ye'll 'ave t' pay!" he answered surlily.

"I am prepared to do that."

Orlena alighted and walked through the open half of the door to find herself amongst the props, ropes, and animal cages which she had seen the night Terry had taken her behind the stage.

A man in shirt-sleeves was sitting on an upturned box, mopping the sweat from his brow with a dirty rag.

"Excuse me," Orlena said, "I wonder if you could tell me if Miss Jenny Stevens is here?"

The man jerked his thumb towards the stage.

"Out front," he replied gruffly.

Orlena followed the direction in which he pointed and found herself on the stage.

The curtains were drawn back and she looked across the empty Orchestra-pit to see Jenny and Snowball in the ring.

The letters of the alphabet were spread out and the pianoforte was being played while Snowball pawed them.

Orlena found the steps which led from the stage into the auditorium, and as she climbed down them and went towards Jenny she heard her say crossly:

"No! That is useless! Play the note C firmly, so that Snowball can understand, but not so that it is obvious to the audience."

Orlena drew nearer and she saw that the pianist sitting at the pianoforte was not the man whom Jenny had referred to as Pat, but a much older man who was peering through spectacles at the music propped up in front of him.

"Miss Stevens!" Orlena said nervously.

Jenny turned round and stared at her, obviously not recognising her.

"I am Orlena Weldon—Terry's sister."

"Oh, of course," Jenny cried, smiling and holding out her hand. "I've not seen you in a bonnet before —and a very becoming one, if I may say so."

"I . . . want your help," Orlena said.

"In what way?" Jenny asked.

"I can see you are busy rehearsing," Orlena said. "I will wait, if you want me to."

"No, no. Tell me what it's all about," Jenny replied. "Has Terry sent you?"

"No . . . Terry does not know I am here," Orlena answered, feeling embarrassed because Terry was no longer interested in this attractive woman.

Jenny certainly looked different now from when she was dressed in her white ballet-dress with a wreath of white roses in her hair.

She was wearing a nondescript, rather dirty gown, short so that Orlena could see her ballet-shoes, with nothing glamorous or even smart about it.

Her golden hair was dragged back into a bun at the base of her neck, and without make-up she looked older.

"What I came to . . . ask you," Orlena said hesitatingly, "was if you could help me find . . . employment playing the piano. I realise there would be no vacancies here . . . but perhaps you might know of . . . somewhere else."

Jenny looked at her in surprise and she explained:

"Terry and I thought we had inherited a lot of . . . money . . . but it was a mistake . . . and we have . . .

nothing except a pile of . . . debts which have to be paid."

"That's bad luck!" Jenny said sympathetically.

"I . . . could think of no-one who could . . . help me, except you," Orlena explained, "and I can play the pianoforte very well."

"You can? How well?" Jenny asked.

Orlena felt it was the professional being suspicious of the amateur and said quickly without thinking:

"Far better than Pat at any rate!"

"So you remember Pat," Jenny said. "Well, he's let me down and pretty badly at that!"

"What has he done?" Orlena enquired.

"Got blind drunk last week after the show, smashed a shop-window with an empty bottle, and now he's in the clink!"

"Do you mean in prison?" Orlena asked.

"Yes, and I've got to find another pianist by to-night."

Orlena's eyes widened and the two women looked at each other.

"You couldn't be worse than the old fool I'm try-ing out at this moment," Jenny said. "Do you want to have a go and see what you can do?"

"May I?" Orlena asked.

"Take off your bonnet and get down to it," Jenny said. "We've little enough time!"

Chapter Six

Snowball was pawing with a hoof at the letters and Jenny was keeping up the patter with which Orlena was now familiar.

She had learnt after nine performances that Snowball's repertoire was in fact very limited.

When Jenny turned to the audience and asked them to suggest a word, if possible of three letters so that more people could have a choice, she actually chose the word herself.

There had been a dozen voices distinctive above the roar of the others, but Jenny had pointed to the far end of the auditorium.

"Did I hear you say 'hat,' Sir? Yes, 'hat'! Snowball will spell that for you; and I am sure it will be becoming if you put it on the side of your dark, handsome head!"

This caused a roar of laughter and no-one in fact realised that the word "hat" had come from Jenny and not from any member of the audience.

This of course gave Orlena time to choose the music with which Snowball was familiar, and to accentuate the notes which told the horse which letter to choose.

Snowball was very intelligent and, what was

more, Orlena was certain that he enjoyed the performance.

There was no doubt that there was a deep love between Jenny and her mount. Whenever she appeared in the field where Snowball was grazing he would gallop up to her and nuzzle at her adoringly while she talked to him and petted him.

"How long have you been doing this act?" Orlena asked.

"I would not like to tell you how many years," Jenny answered. "I started with my father when I was a little girl. We had a different horse then, although he was not as good as Snowball. Later, when my father died, he had trained Snowball so well that he will now do almost anything I ask of him."

She patted the white horse's neck, then laid her cheeks against his mane in a gesture of affection which Orlena found very touching.

On the first night that she had played for Jenny and Snowball it had been so nerve-wracking that afterwards she would often wake up in the night dreaming of it and knowing that it had been worse than a nightmare.

When Jenny had suggested that she should see what she could do, she had paid off the hackney-carriage.

Then taking off her cloak and hat, Orlena had sat down at the piano feeling that it would be impossible for her fingers to play the tunes which were wanted.

But, as always, the mere sound of music, whatever it was, brought with it a sense of serenity and with every note she played she grew more confident.

This feeling was helped by the knowledge that the grand pianoforte on which she played was one of the latest developed by John Broadwood.

"Astley's believes in buying the best," Jenny replied when Orlena commented on it. "That's why his horses are outstanding."

The pianoforte was a fine instrument and a great improvement on the Viennese one on which Orlena had played at home and which for the last years her father had refused to have tuned.

It was a joy to use the "loud" and "soft" pedals and to hear the strength, sonority, and brilliance of the notes.

But however much Orlena longed to be carried away by the music she made, she had to watch Snowball and at the same time be quick enough to pick out the tune which was required. But after two hours Jenny had clapped her hands.

"You are splendid!" she cried. "Quite splendid! A far better pianist than anyone I have ever had before!"

"You mean . . . I am engaged?" Orlena asked.

"Of course you are," Jenny replied. "That is—if you are really serious in saying you need a job."

"I do need it," Orlena answered. "At the same time, I must find somewhere to stay."

For the first time it seemed that Jenny, intent on her own problems, considered Orlena's.

"You mean you can't stay with Terry?" she asked.

"Terry must not know I am here," Orlena answered quickly. "That is important, Jenny."

She saw that Jenny was going to ask questions, and added:

"I do not want to discuss the reason, but I must disguise myself somehow. Perhaps I could wear spectacles or a veil over my face."

Jenny looked at her reflectively, then after a moment she said:

"I have an idea. If you really mean you do not wish to be recognised, then we can disguise you completely."

"How?" Orlena asked a little nervously.

She had a sudden vision of being covered in grease-paint like a clown.

"I know that in the wardrobe there's a very

pretty costume of a Venetian Lady, and part of the costume is a mask."

Orlena gave a little cry.

"How clever of you, Jenny! Of course that is exactly what I need, a mask over my eyes so that no-one will recognise me."

The costume when she saw it was even more effective than she had anticipated.

There was not only the little black mask edged with lace to hide her face, but the traditional lace veil which completely covered her hair under a smart velvet tricorn hat.

The dress was red and although Orlena knew that it was made of a cheap material and the embroidery on it was very roughly done, from the audience it looked extremely luxurious and glamorous.

When she had put it on and it had been altered slightly to fit her very slim waist, she thought that no-one, not even Terry, would recognise her.

Even as she thought of him she knew that it was not Terry of whom she was afraid, but someone very different.

Then she told herself she was being needlessly apprehensive.

It was very unlikely that the Earl would ever condescend to visit Astley's Amphitheatre and he certainly would not suspect her of being a pianist for one of the equestrian turns.

When they had finished rehearsing and deciding upon her gown, there was very little time before they had to be ready for the evening performance.

"I do not want to be a nuisance," Orlena said humbly to Jenny, "but I must find somewhere to stay tonight."

"I'll look after you," Jenny replied good-humouredly. "You mightn't find it very posh, but you can come to my 'digs' this evening at any rate. I know Ma's got an empty room at the back. It's little more than a cupboard, but at least you'll be safe from the 'Roving Romeos'!"

Orlena had not at the time understood what this implied.

She was to learn in the next two or three nights that there were always men of every sort and kind waiting after a performance to ask those who had taken part in it out to supper.

She knew that if she had not been with Jenny she would in fact have been very frightened of them.

Sometimes they were drunk and aggressive, sometimes they were looking for a very different type of amusement from what was provided by the Circus.

They would come along the passage on which the dressing-rooms opened, peeping through the doors and making a general nuisance of themselves, and there was really nothing to stop them.

Jenny managed them firmly and with a determination which evoked Orlena's sincere admiration.

At the same time, she was grateful for her mask, finding it wiser to keep it on until even the most persistent Romeo had left the Amphitheatre.

There were a lot of things for Orlena to learn about in the next few days.

The room which Jenny had procured for her in the house where she lodged was certainly small and uncomfortable, and the dirty window let in very little air.

But Orlena knew that she would never be able to manage on her own and was only too grateful to Jenny for keeping her under her protection.

Their landlady was a red-faced blousy woman with an addiction to gin, but she was good-natured and willing to cook them something for their supper after the performance, provided they paid her.

Orlena thought that anyone as attractive as Jenny would be asked out to supper every night of the week, but she was to learn that this was not the case.

Although there were undoubtedly men only too

eager to buy her a meal, they considered this only a preliminary to demanding other favours, and she refused them with a sharpness and an authority which Orlena envied.

"I miss seeing your brother," Jenny said once wistfully.

Orlena felt embarrassed that Terry should have transferred his affections so quickly to the Opera Dancer.

"Do you ever see Lord Westover?" she asked quickly, so as to divert the conversation from Terry.

Jenny shook her head.

"He never came back after that night when we all went out together to dinner. I thought he was seeing you."

"No, I did not see him again," Orlena answered.

"It seems strange," Jenny reflected. "He was taken with you—I was sure of that!"

Orlena could not help thinking that if Lord Westover knew the position she was in now, he might wish to renew their acquaintance.

But she had a feeling that he, like Terry and the Earl, would be very shocked at what she was doing and be determined to remove her from the Circus immediately.

It was not only her place of work and her lodgings which Orlena found so strange: the streets themselves, now that she was walking and not driving, took on a very different appearance.

They were of course thronged with hackney-coaches, private carriages, calashes, Phaetons, barouches, Post-Chaises, and mail-coaches, which she had seen before from the Earl's carriage.

But now she noticed the Twopenny Postmen with their bells, the lamplighters, the scavengers, the cadgers, the Jewish mendicants, the horse-copers, the herb women, and the ragged barefooted children.

These would cluster round the Saloop-stall near

the Circus and, not being able to afford to buy a bowl, would sniff its fumes.

Careful though she knew she must be of her money, Orlena could not resist paying the three-halfpence which a Saloop cost.

It was an infusion of sassafras, sugar, and milk, and she learnt it was the favourite dinner of the poor, unhappy, and ill-treated little chimney-sweep boys.

It was only when she was alone at night in the small truckle bed, with its torn, thin blankets and hard straw pillow, that Orlena allowed herself to think of the Earl.

It was then that her love for him swept over her like a tidal wave and she would feel herself quiver as she remembered his kiss in the garden of the Bushel and what it had meant to her.

Just sometimes, when she was waiting for the stage-hands to push the pianoforte into the ring, she would play softly the first notes of the music which she had composed that night.

It brought the Earl so vividly to her mind that she felt almost as if he stood beside her.

It was not only the touch of his lips that she longed for and which made her whole body ache, but the expression in his eyes, his twisted smile, even the cynical lines on his face and the mocking note in his voice.

"I love him! I love him!" she would cry despairingly, and wondered miserably if he ever thought of her kindly or if he was merely incensed because she had run away.

He would never understand, she thought, that she had gone because she owed him so much money and could not bear to be in his debt, whatever she owed to other people.

He had despised her from the very beginning.

The only way she could reinstate herself, if only just a little, in his estimation was to pay him back, however long it took, the thousand pounds she had given away without consulting him.

It made it worse that she had given it so impulsively without realising how much he was already doing personally for the children she pitied.

"I have been so foolish in so many ways," Orlena told herself.

Then she could only tremble at the thought of the Earl's anger and the look of contempt on his face when he had accused her of giving money to some fortune-hunter.

He had apologised, it was true.

But that could not erase the hurt because he had thought her capable of deception and of behaving in a manner which would have been contrary to all her ideals and to what she knew was right.

Everything had gone wrong, she thought helplessly, from the moment he had kissed her in the garden.

It was because she had been unable to struggle against him or behave as any woman of propriety should have done. It had been impossible.

His lips had held hers captive, and the feeling of wonder and rapture which had swept over her was too compelling, too marvellous, to resist.

She had surrendered herself to it because she found it impossible to do anything else, but how could she explain that to him?

How could she make him realise that it was not something she would have done with any other man, but only with him, with him alone?

Snowball had spelt out the word "hat" and was now pawing the letter C for "cot."

Automatically, it seemed, Orlena played the right music, though she was deep in her thoughts, hardly conscious of what was happening round her.

She was trying not to think of the Earl, trying to concentrate on the act, but somehow she could feel his presence so vividly that she felt in sudden terror that he must be in the audience.

Of course it was impossible! Why should he come to a place like this?

It was true that quite a number of fashionable gentlemen did condescend to visit the Amphitheatre because they admired the horsemanship of the riders.

But the trick-riding, interspersed with the vulgarity of the clowns, the dancing dogs, and the performing bears, was hardly something which would interest the Earl.

Orlena told herself she was just being imaginative. And even if he was there, he would not recognise her.

At her first performances she had been vividly conscious of the audience round her and through the slits in her mask she would even at times look towards the boxes, afraid lest she should see a familiar face.

Then when she realised how anonymous she was in her Venetian costume she ceased to be so self-conscious.

There was always one moment of embarrassment and that was when she had to follow the pianoforte into the ring, walking behind the men who pushed it, aware that some people at any rate in the packed Amphitheatre were looking at her.

But the vast majority were concerned only with Jenny, who having pirouetted on Snowball's back made him bow to the applause.

He did it very gracefully, putting out first his right front leg and bending his head almost to the ground, then his left leg.

The applause took some time and by the time it was dying away the pianoforte was in place and Orlena was seated on the stool.

The Orchestra, which had played during the first part of Jenny's act, shuffled away under the stage and now there was only the melody from the piano to be heard.

Orlena played loudly for a few moments, then softened the sound until it almost died away as the alphabet was laid out in front of Snowball and Jenny began to explain to the audience that he would now show how well he could read.

"One more word," Jenny was saying now.

There were shouts from all over the Amphitheatre, some of them rather coarse, some far too long and too ludicrous, but Jenny had everything in hand.

"Did I hear you say 'Bob'?" she asked, pointing to the back of the Gallery. "Well, I'll bet you a bob that Snowball doesn't make a mistake, and if he does, I'll pay you, though with my salary it might take me months to do so!"

There was laughter at this, but Orlena was already playing the tune with which Snowball was familiar. The horse moved towards the letter B and began to paw it with his hoof.

"That's right—B!" Jenny shouted. "Come on, Snowball, find O for 'orange.' "

Obediently Snowball moved towards the end of the long line of the alphabet and found the right letter.

"Bo," Jenny cried, "and Bo to you, Sir, for doubting that Snowball would win a 'Bob' for me! Don't forget to bring it round to my dressing-room later, or I promise you I'll set the duns on you."

She patted Snowball.

"One more B, Snowball, and whatever the gentleman brings you'll get half! I only hope it's something *you'll* enjoy!"

She gave a mischievous glance at the audience, who laughed again.

Then as Orlena struck the note for the letter B determinedly on the piano and Snowball moved towards it, there was a sudden cry from the stage.

It was so loud and so shrill that instinctively Jenny turned her head.

The cry came again and this time it was quite distinct:

"Fire! Fire!"

There was an audible gasp from the audience, then pandemonium broke out and as it did so the curtains on the stage burst into flame.

Flames crept up the sides and flames appeared in the centre and there was the smell of burning.

It all happened so suddenly that Orlena could only sit at the piano, staring in astonishment.

Then she realised that the whole Amphitheatre had gone crazy and the noise was deafening.

People were shouting, screaming, climbing over the wooden benches and knocking them and one another over as they rushed for the exits.

She saw Jenny fling herself onto Snowball's back, gallop across the ring, leap the surrounding rail, and vanish into the seething crowd.

Orlena rose to her feet and stood where she was, holding on to the pianoforte. It gave her in fact protection from being knocked over.

Now from behind the stage there came a crowd of people and animals.

The dancing dogs seemed to drag their trainers with them. The bear came ambling along on all fours beside his keeper, who held a chain which encircled his neck.

There were a number of stage-hands all yelling at the tops of their voices as they ran through the ring.

The noise and confusion was increased by the fact that the lights which lit the Amphitheatre had become extinguished and now in the auditorium there were only the flames from the fire to show the way.

People seemed to loom like dark shadows upon Orlena, and banging against the pianoforte so that it heaved and moved like a living thing, they passed on to join the general mêlée fighting for the exits.

Women were screaming continuously and men were shouting.

Orlena looked over her shoulder, far too afraid to move away, at the same time conscious that the flames on the stage were leaping higher and had now reached the roof.

There was not only the smell of burning but also the penetrating smoke, which made it hard to breathe.

She pulled off her mask and as she did so a man bumped into her so violently that her tricorn hat fell from her head.

She gave a little cry which seemed even to herself to be strangled in her throat.

'I must get out of this,' she thought, but had no idea how she could do so.

There seemed to be people everywhere and the noise in the Amphitheatre seemed to grow more deafening and more frightening.

The fire was doing a great deal of damage.

Now she could hear the sound of falling beams, or perhaps it was the scenery behind the stage, and the flames enveloped the Orchestra-pit.

They began to creep along the Amphitheatre itself, reaching the stage-boxes and consuming the red plush curtains which seemed so garishly gay.

"I must get away," Orlena said to herself.

Yet it seemed dangerous to leave the protection of the pianoforte and she knew that she was trembling with the fear of being knocked down and being unconscious on the sawdust of the ring.

She could see other women falling and realised that men were letting themselves down by their hands from the Gallery.

They dropped into the crowd below them, and, judging by the noise and screams, damaged other people as they did so.

Orlena looked first one way, then the other, and knew despairingly that the flames were advancing along the boxes and the benches on the ground near the stage faster than the people were able to leave the Amphitheatre.

"What shall I do?" she cried in terror.

Then suddenly someone picked her up and she gave a little scream.

"It is all right," a familiar voice said. "I will take care of you."

For a moment Orlena was stunned into silence.

Then as she knew who held her she felt her heart give a leap of sheer happiness and the terror she had felt was gone.

She was safe! He had found her!

He had come when she most needed him! She need make no decisions but to leave herself completely in his hands.

He was moving, she thought, towards one of the crowded exits, but she did not bother to look.

She merely turned her face against his shoulder and thought she had never been so happy in her whole life.

This is what she had wanted, what she had ached and yearned for every night; this is what she had prayed for and thought would never happen.

But he had found her and somehow there were no more problems, no more fear, no more danger.

She could still hear the screams and shouts of the audience, the noise and crackle of the flames, and the smoke was still making it hard for her to breathe, but none of it mattered.

She could hide her face against him, feel his arms holding her very close against his heart.

'I love him!' Orlena thought. 'I love him and nothing else is of any consequence.'

Actually it took some time for the Earl to move slowly but relentlessly through the crowd.

He looked round him.

Men were fighting their way towards the exits
and women were falling to the ground to be trampled
underfoot.

But because he kept his head and chose his way
with care and was in fact taller and stronger than
most of the people round him, the Earl emerged at
one of the side entrances to the Amphitheatre which
led into the field.

He walked quickly away from the crowds milling
round the burning building and crossed the whole
length of the field before he turned towards the road.

Only when he reached the boundary fence did
he turn to look back to see the Amphitheatre, a burning beacon against the darkening sky.

The ships' timbers, the canvas roof, and the wood
with which the rest of the theatre was built were
fuel for the advancing flames, and the fire now had
such a grip on the building that it was obvious no-
one was making the least effort to save it.

The fields at the back where the Earl was standing were filled with frightened animals getting as far
away as they could from the fire.

The Earl looked towards them, then turned in
the opposite direction towards Westminster Bridge
Road.

He found a place in the wall that was easily
negotiable and now he put Orlena down on her feet.

She stood swaying uncertainly, and he thought
that her eyes must have been closed while she hid
her face against his shoulder.

"We will have to climb over this wall," he explained. "I will lift you up and place you on top of
it, then I will climb it myself and lift you down on
the other side."

She looked up at him and he could see her face
framed by the Venetian lace veil in the light from
the flames. Her eyes held a radiance which was unmistakable and she was no longer afraid.

He looked at her for a long moment, his arms

still supporting her. Then resolutely he picked her up again and placed her on top of the wall, steadying her for a moment.

"You are all right?" he asked.

She did not answer and he knew she was finding it hard to speak. Then he climbed over the wall and lifted her down on the other side.

She was very soft and yielding in his arms and he did not, as she expected, put her down again but carried her a little way along the road to where he thought his carriage would be waiting.

He was not mistaken.

There were his magnificent pair of horses in the light from the fire and his coachman and footman looking anxiously for him, and he saw the relief on their faces as they watched his approach.

"Thank God you're all right, M'Lord," the coachman said. "We were wondering what we should best do."

"You did quite right to stay where you were," the Earl replied.

The footman opened the door of the carriage and the Earl lifted Orlena inside and set her down on the back seat.

Then he climbed in after her.

The horses started off and as if she was unable to prevent herself Orlena turned towards him and hid her face against his shoulder.

His arms went round her and he held her very close.

"You ... saved ... me!" she said in a very small voice.

It was the first sound she had made since she had given a cry of terror as the Earl had picked her up in his arms.

He did not speak and after a moment she said, her voice muffled against his coat:

"H-how ... did you ... find me? How did you ... know it was ... me?"

She thought that the Earl's arms tightened before he said:

"How could you have done anything so crazy, so utterly insane, as to run away?"

The elation she had felt because she was close to him seemed suddenly menaced.

Now Orlena was frightened that he would be angry and he felt her body go tense before she answered in a hesitating little voice:

"I . . . I wanted to . . . pay you back . . . what I . . . owed you."

"That is something you can never do," the Earl replied.

Orlena gave a little sigh.

"I . . . know it is a lot of money, b-but I did want . . . to try. I . . . I was so ashamed of being so . . . foolish."

"It is not money you have cost me," the Earl said. "It is desperate worry and anxiety, sleepless nights. Do you realise what chaos you left behind you, Orlena?"

She was so surprised at his words that she raised her head to look at him, seeking his face in the faint light shining through the darkness from the oil lamps and the link-men's torches.

But it was hard to see him clearly although he was looking at her, and because she was certain he was angry she felt herself tremble.

"I could not believe you had really left," he said in a voice she found it difficult to recognise, "and when Terry showed me your letter I became frantic with anxiety."

"I was . . . quite safe," Orlena said in a very low voice.

"How could I be sure of that?" the Earl asked sharply. "How could I be sure of anything except that you had gone?"

He pulled her a little closer to him as he said:

"It was not only a foolish thing for you to do,

but also a wicked one. I do not remember ever being so anxious as I have been this past week, with my mother in tears and Terry behaving like a madman!"

There was so much accusation in his voice that Orlena felt the tears come into her own eyes.

"I am sorry . . . I am sorry," she murmured. "I did not . . . mean to be any . . . trouble. I just wanted to . . . do what was right."

"Right! How could you think it right to run away, knowing nothing about London? Leaving us distraught with worry as to what might have happened to you?"

"I . . . I am . . . sorry," Orlena whispered again.

"And what do you think would have happened tonight if I had not been there?" the Earl asked.

Orlena did not answer and he said in a scolding tone she knew so well:

"How could you have coped alone in that crowd? You would surely have lost your life."

Now there was a note in his voice that made her heart throb in a strange way.

It was almost, she thought, as if he really cared, as if he would have minded if she had died.

Because she could not bear him to be angry with her she said passionately:

"Please . . . forgive me . . . I am sorry . . . very sorry if I have done anything wrong, but I could not . . . owe you all that . . . money and not try to re-pay it. It was . . . your money I had given away so . . . stupidly . . . and there was nothing else I . . . could do but try to be . . . honest about it."

"You do not owe me any money," the Earl said.

"B-but . . . one thousand pounds!"

He made a sound of exasperation as he said:

"If you could only have waited a little while instead of tearing off in that absurd way, you would have learnt that your father's Bonds had been found and that you were in fact not giving my money to the Vicar of St. James's—but your own!"

"They ... they have been found?" Orlena murmured almost incoherently.

"This should teach you, if nothing else, not to read letters that were not meant for you," the Earl said reprovingly.

"But ... how? How could they have been missing in the first place?" Orlena asked.

"Your father took them from the Bank for some unknown reason of his own and put them into a secret cupboard in his bed-room."

"B-but they were not there ... I am sure they were not there!" Orlena said.

"What you did not know," the Earl explained, "was that there is a false panel in the cupboard with another secret hiding-place beyond it. It had originally, I think, been a Priests' Hole, and the secret of it was passed from father to son. That was why you had no knowledge of it."

"So ... Terry knew?" Orlena asked weakly.

"Yes, Terry knew," the Earl said. "When I told him what had happened, he suggested that Mr. Thorogood should look in the hiding-place beyond the cupboard, and there the Bonds were found."

"Oh, I am glad, so very glad for Terry's sake," Orlena gasped.

She drew in a deep breath of relief.

"And so I do not ... owe you anything ... after all."

"No, you owe me a great deal!" the Earl said sternly.

She looked at him in surprise.

"B-but ... how ... ?"

"You owe me for all I have suffered when I thought I had lost you," he said. "That has to be repaid."

"I ... I do not ... think I ... understand," she said hesitatingly.

At the same time, because of the way he had

spoken, her heart had begun beating frantically and she felt as if something strange had happened to her throat so that it was hard to speak.

"How could you have dared to make me suffer like this?" the Earl asked.

Now the anger in his voice was combined with a strange music that had begun to play in her heart.

He pulled her closer still. Then his lips were on hers and she knew that this was what she had been longing for and praying for ever since he had last kissed her.

It was all the rapture and wonder she had known in the garden, yet now there was something deeper and more wonderful in the touch of his mouth.

It was as if before he had taken her up to the very gates of Heaven, but now they were open and he took her inside.

Everything was golden with a glory that was almost unbearable and there was celestial music playing that linked them together in a manner that was indescribable.

Her lips were very soft and defenceless and she felt as if he drew not only her heart from between them but her soul and her mind, so that she was no longer herself but a part of him.

It was so exquisite, so perfect, so wonderful that she felt as if she could no longer breathe or think, but only quiver with a thousand wonders that were inexpressible.

The Earl raised his head.

"My darling—my foolish, ridiculous little darling! How could I ever lose you? How could you ever leave me?"

"I . . . love you!"

Orlena's words seemed to come from very far away even to herself, and yet there was nothing else to say, nothing in the whole world—except love.

He looked down at her for a moment, then he

was kissing her again, kissing her slowly, possessively, and passionately in a manner which made her whole body quiver and move against his.

The carriage seemed to be full of stars and the wonder of them was blinding.

Only as they drew up outside Ulverston House did the Earl's arms loosen round Orlena and slowly, as if by a superhuman effort, they drew a little away from each other.

A footman opened the door.

The Earl stepped out first, then helped Orlena to alight, and with his arm protectively round her he drew her in through the front door.

The Butler came forward.

"You have found Miss Orlena, M'Lord! That's good news—very good!"

"Yes, I have found her, Bateson," the Earl replied, "but we have just come through a very unpleasant experience, and we would like something to eat and drink."

"There are sandwiches in the Library, M'Lord."

"Tell the Chef we require supper in half an hour," the Earl said.

"Very good, M'Lord."

The Butler hurried ahead to open the Library door and the Earl drew Orlena into the big book-lined room.

She felt that with its deep sofas, silver sconces, and rows of colourful bindings it held a familiar welcome. Then as the door closed she had eyes only for the man who had followed her into the room.

She turned to look at him, and at the expression on his face she gave a little cry of sheer happiness and ran into his arms.

He held her close for a moment, then he was kissing her again, kissing her wildly, frantically, passionately, until the walls of the Library spun dizzily round.

Orlena felt as though they both melted in the

heat of the flames they had left behind and that she
was burning with an ecstasy that was ignited by the
touch of the Earl's lips.

                    *   *   *

As Orlena finished supper she looked at the Earl
and gave a little laugh.

"I had forgotten how delicious food could be,"
she said. "I am so tired—I cannot tell you how tired
—of pigs' trotters and sausages, and stews made with
some very strange ingredients."

"I refuse to say again that it was your own fault,"
the Earl replied, "and that you got all you deserved!"

"You have made me very ... conscious of my ...
misdeeds," Orlena answered.

He rose from his seat at the head of the table
to help her from her chair.

"Come into the Library," he said. "I want to talk
to you."

She looked at him a little anxiously and he said:

"I am not angry, if that is what makes you afraid."

"I am not ... afraid," she answered, "not ... really."

As if she could not help herself she suddenly put
her face against his shoulder in a little gesture of
endearment which made the Earl tighten his arms
round her.

He kissed her hair, then drew her from the small
Dining-Room in which they had eaten, down the passage towards the Library.

Only as they reached it did Orlena say hesitatingly:

"I felt when I went up to ... change that it
was ... too late to ... disturb your mother, but
ought we not tell the ... Duchess that I am ...
back?"

"The Duchess has left," the Earl answered.

Orlena looked at him and he explained:

"That was one of the things I was going to talk
to you about."

Orlena suddenly felt as if an icy hand clutched at her heart.

In the joy of being with the Earl again she had forgotten about Lady Adelaide. She had in fact forgotten everything but him, because he filled her whole world.

Now she remembered what had happened before she left Ulverston House and how Lady Adelaide had told her she was to marry the Earl and that she was of no consequence in his life.

He had kissed her and given her the unutterable glory she had known before, but that, as she well knew, meant little to him.

Now she told herself that once again she had been too easy and had obviously behaved in a manner in which no well-brought-up young lady should have done.

She had gone upstairs before supper and changed from her theatrical costume into one of the pretty gowns hanging in the wardrobe where she had left them.

A maid had attended to her, but it had not been Nicholls, because the head house-maid, being elderly, had retired to bed. So, not liking to ask questions, Orlena had learnt nothing of what had happened at Ulverston House since she had left.

Besides, she had been in too much of a hurry to return to the Earl—to be with him as she longed to be.

But now, she told herself, she had to face the truth, however unpalatable it might be, however unhappy it might make her.

She had to return to the place she had previously occupied—as the Earl's Ward, who could mean little else in his life.

Yet, because she loved him, because even to be beside him was to thrill and feel as if her whole body vibrated to him, she looked at him with wide eyes as the door of the Library closed behind them.

Instinctively she moved towards the hearth-rug, although because it was a warm evening there was no fire but only an exquisite arrangement of flowers to fill the fire-place.

She stood waiting and he walked across the room after her.

She felt as if they were both moving to music which was somehow intermingled with the fragrance of lilies.

The Earl reached her side and did not speak but stood looking down at her.

His eyes seemed to search her face, those penetrating dark eyes of which she had been so afraid, but which now she loved because they were his.

Because she felt shy at his scrutiny she said after a moment:

"You . . . you were . . . telling me about . . . the Duchess."

"She has gone back to the country," the Earl answered, "and while you are of course chaperoned by my mother, I cannot be sure, because she is still ill, that she will look after you adequately."

"I promise I will do nothing of which you will . . . disapprove," Orlena said quickly.

"How can I be certain of that unless I look after you myself?"

She stared at him a little puzzled. Then he said very quietly:

"I am asking you to marry me, Orlena!"

For a moment she was still, feeling she could not have heard what he said.

"B-but you are to . . . marry Lady Adelaide."

"I never had any intention of marrying Lady Adelaide," the Earl said. "That was an idea thought up by my mother and the Duchess. In fact, if you want the truth, Orlena, I had no intention of marrying anyone."

He paused and his smile twisted his lips.

"Not even you, my precious."

"Then ... why ... ?" Orlena began in a bewildered way.

"I told myself I wished to be free—to live a bachelor life because it suited me—but I do not intend to suffer again as you have made me suffer this past week," the Earl answered. "Nor can I again spend my valuable time scouring the Music Centres of London, some of which are extremely disreputable, in the hope of finding a girl whose one salable talent is that she can play the pianoforte."

"You have done that?"

"I think I have visited every damned Concert-Hall, every Teaching Academy, every Music Club in the entire city!" the Earl said sharply.

She guessed how much he would have disliked it.

"I ... I am ... sorry."

"It was only today that Terry confessed to me that he had taken you to Astley's Amphitheatre," the Earl went on. "We were both thinking about places connected with music and it struck him—rather belatedly—that there was music at a Circus!"

"So you came to ... see if I was there."

"As soon as Terry told me that you liked the woman to whom he had introduced you, I was quite certain that was where I would find you," the Earl said.

"You were not ... angry with Terry?"

"I intended to be very angry with him for introducing you to such a person," the Earl replied, "but now I can only be grateful that he directed me to the right place—and at the right moment."

Orlena thought of the fire and shuddered.

The Earl's arms went round her.

"Fate sent me to find you—not Terry," he said. "He could not have known that the damned place would go on fire for the second time."

He held her closer still as he said in a voice she hardly recognised:

"I promise you one thing, my darling, never again in your life will I allow you to visit such a place."

It was difficult for Orlena to think or speak when she was so close to him, but she had to ask the question:

"Do you ... really want to ... marry me?"

"I intend to marry you," the Earl replied. "As your Guardian I recommend myself as being extremely eligible, and most certainly not a fortune-hunter! As far as I am concerned, you can give away every penny you own."

Orlena drew in her breath, but her eyes were still on his face, seeking what she wanted to hear.

As if he knew instinctively what she asked, the Earl bent his head and his lips were very close to hers as he said:

"I love you, my darling! I love you as I have never loved any woman in my life before—in fact I cannot live without you! Is that what you want me to say?"

Then there was no need for words.

There was only music, the magic of the stars, and a wonder of wonders as his lips met hers.

Chapter Seven

The Earl opened the communicating door between his bed-room and the one which had always been occupied by the Countess of Ulverston.

The room was in darkness save for two candles, and as he approached the huge silk-curtained bed with its canopy of carved golden doves he realised it was empty.

It was then that he heard strains of music coming from the *Boudoir* on the far side of the room.

There was a smile on his face as he walked towards it, wondering how many bridegrooms had found their brides not waiting for them but playing the pianoforte.

He and Orlena had been married that morning at St. James's, Westminster.

It had been a quiet wedding with only their immediate relatives present, because the Prince had already left for Brighton and most of the *Beau Ton* had either followed him or retired to their country Estates.

That she need not have a huge Society Wedding saved Orlena from feeling nervous, and it also pleased the Earl, who disliked social occasions of that sort.

The Church was decorated with white flowers,

and as Orlena came up the aisle on Terry's arm she looked, the Earl had thought, like a flower herself.

There was something very young, very innocent and pure about her face under the transparent veil, and he knew that this was what he had always sought in his wife but never expected to find.

He had been disillusioned so often by women who had pursued him for his title and his wealth that he had come to the conclusion that what he sought was unobtainable.

After the wedding the Earl and Orlena drove in his Phaeton to Ulverston Park in Kent.

As they set out behind his team of four magnificent chestnuts, Orlena said with a lilt in her voice:

"This is exciting! I have so often wanted to drive with you."

The Earl turned his head to smile at her as she went on:

"But you never asked me, and I was so jealous of Lady Adelaide when I knew that you took her with you in the Park."

"I wanted you with me," the Earl said, "but I was doing my best not to become too involved."

"You are not . . . sorry now that you . . . are?" Orlena asked.

"I will answer that question when I do not have to concentrate on my horses—unless you wish to be involved in an accident!"

There was a note in his voice which gave her the answer without words and she made a little sound that was one of sheer happiness.

"I have so much to show you in my home," the Earl went on, "and when you are bored with that we can always go elsewhere for the rest of our honeymoon."

"Do you really think I could ever be bored with you?" Orlena asked.

He smiled at her again and she thought how

much younger he looked since they had become engaged.

There was no longer that cynical expression on his face which she had noticed the very first time she had seen him, and when he was talking to her he forgot to drawl.

They reached Ulverston Park and for a moment as they went down the drive Orlena was stunned into silence.

She had expected anything that belonged to the Earl to be impressive, but not to be so large, so magnificent, and so awe-inspiringly beautiful.

"It is . . . too big!" she said almost to herself. "I am . . . frightened!"

"You need never be frightened when you are with me," the Earl replied. "I have told you that I will look after you, Orlena, and I intend to do so for the rest of my life."

She felt a thrill ripple through her and longed to be in his arms.

They dined not in the huge Baronial Dining-Hall where a hundred people could be seated with ease, but in a small oval room that had been added to the house by Adam.

It was decorated with exquisite statuary of Greek goddesses, their perfect bodies seeming to the Earl to resemble Orlena's.

He was delighted with her wide-eyed appreciation of everything she saw, and he told himself there were many happy hours ahead in which he would show her his home, his grounds, and his many other possessions.

There was no time to see anything much that evening, and when Orlena had gone up the staircase to retire for the night the Earl knew he was as impatient to be with her as any young man with his first love.

Now he walked silently into the *Boudoir* and saw his wife sitting at the white Broadwood piano which on his instructions had been delivered only a few days ago.

It was the very latest and most up-to-date model pianoforte in the world. He had known that Orlena would appreciate it, but he had not expected her to discover it so soon.

He stood just inside the doorway.

She was sitting at the pianoforte, the only light coming from a large silver candelabra in which six lighted candles flickered very slightly in the breeze from the open window.

It was a hot night and Orlena was wearing only a thin, white lawn nightgown, with her hair falling over her shoulders almost to her waist.

She looked very lovely, very ethereal, and the music she played seemed to the Earl to have something spiritual about it that he had not heard before.

He walked across the room and only as he reached her did Orlena look up and he saw by the light of the candles the happiness in her eyes.

She would have risen, but he said quickly:

"Go on playing. I know, Orlena, that you talk to me through your music, and I will try to be as intelligent as Snowball."

Orlena gave a little laugh but she did not cease playing.

"Jenny is afraid that as you have been kind enough to give Snowball a home until the Amphitheatre opens again, he will grow so fat and happy that he will forget all his tricks."

"I see that we shall have to rehearse him occasionally," the Earl smiled.

"It was very generous of you to have him here," Orlena said, "and even more generous to send Jenny for a holiday for the sea. She told me that she has never seen the sea."

"I would have sent her anywhere in the world she wished to go," the Earl replied. "I shall always be grateful to her for having kept you safe and, as you told me yourself, protected you from the 'Roving Romeos.'"

Orlena lowered her eyes and blushed a little, but she went on playing and after a moment the Earl said:

"I believe that is the melody you composed in the garden of the Bushel."

"Only the very beginning of it," Orlena answered. "Afterwards, when I . . . met you, it became very . . . different."

"After I had kissed you," he said softly. "A kiss which neither of us could forget."

"You tried to do so!" Orlena said almost accusingly. "You told me to go back to the North and make some bovine farmer happy."

"Only my sense of direction was wrong," the Earl said. "I should have said South, and I am the bovine farmer whom you will make, my darling Heart, very happy."

He was leaning on the pianoforte to face her as he spoke and she looked up at him in surprise as he added:

"I think you prefer to live in the country, and I personally have had enough of London!"

"Do you really mean that?" Orlena asked.

"There are many things for us to do here together," he replied, "and I think one thing which will please you is that I have decided to build another Orphanage. You shall help to design it."

"That is the most wonderful thing you could do!" Orlena exclaimed.

"Then we will do it together," he answered.

She took her hands from the keys to say:

"How can I thank you? You have made me so . . . happy and there are no . . . words."

"There is always music," the Earl answered, "and that is why, my precious love, I want to see if I can bring you many different melodies now that you are mine and we are married."

"I know you will do that," Orlena said softly.

"Everything about you is so perfect, so part of my dreams and what in the past I have heard in the woods, on the wind and in my heart."

The Earl stood up and putting out his hands drew Orlena from the piano-stool.

"How could I ever have guessed that the girl I met in the garden of the Bushel would be you?" he asked.

"It may have been . . . reprehensible," Orlena said, "but I am glad . . . so very, very glad that Terry took me there."

"I imagine I would have fallen in love with you anyway," the Earl remarked.

"It would not have been the . . . same," she answered. "It was because you kissed me, not knowing who I was, that I was aware in that moment that no other man could ever mean . . . anything to me."

"No other man ever will!" the Earl said positively.

He drew her a little closer as he spoke, feeling the soft warmth of her body through the thin nightgown.

She hardly seemed real, and yet the beating of his heart and the fire burning in his eyes told him that beneath her ethereality there was a woman who attracted him to the point of madness.

And yet, because she was different in every way from the women he had known in the past and because her innocence surrounded her almost like a light, his lips were very gentle as he sought her mouth.

"I love you, my sweet darling!" he said, and felt her move instinctively towards him as a little quiver of excitement went through her.

"I love you!" he went on. "I love you so completely, so absolutely in every way, that I have no wish to frighten you; and so you must teach me, my precious, to be very gentle."

Her head fell back against his shoulder and her eyes looked up into his.

"You . . . excited me the first time I saw you,"

she whispered, "because you were so . . . magnificent and at the same time so overpowering and sure of yourself. I would not wish you to be any . . . different."

The Earl gave a little laugh.

"My sweet! Could there ever be anyone like you?"

His lips became more insistent, more demanding.

Then as Orlena moved even closer to him and he felt the response not only of her mouth but of her whole body, he lifted her in his arms.

* * *

A long, long time later a little voice whispered against the Earl's shoulder:

"I love . . . you!"

"It is impossible for me to express my love for you in words, my adorable little wife!" the Earl replied. "But tell me, my darling, did I bring you music?"

"It was music which was divine and more wonderful than I had imagined possible," Orlena replied.

The Earl's lips moved across her forehead and he kissed her eyes.

"It is a melody that you must play to me," he said, "so that I can never forget the most perfect night of my life."

"It will not be a . . . melody," Orlena answered, feeling herself quiver because his hand was touching her.

He waited for her to explain and she added:

"It will be a . . . rhapsody of wild, indescribable delight because that is what you . . . gave me. That is what is singing in my heart."

"And also in mine," the Earl replied. "A rhapsody of love, my precious darling, which will be with us now and for all eternity."

Then he was kissing her again and there was only the music of their happiness vibrating in the darkness round them.